M for Murder

Shivam Verma

Rajmangal Prakashan

An Imprint of **Rajmangal Publishers**

ISBN : 978-8196299521

Published by :

Rajmangal Publishers

Rajmangal Prakashan Building,
1st Street, Sangwan, Quarsi, Ramghat Road
Aligarh-202001, (UP) INDIA
Cont. No. +91- 7017993445
www.rajmangalpublishers.com
rajmangalpublishers@gmail.com
sampadak@rajmangalpublishers.in

प्रथम संस्करण : अप्रैल 2022 – पेपरबैक

प्रकाशक : राजमंगल प्रकाशन

राजमंगल प्रकाशन बिल्डिंग, 1st स्ट्रीट,

सांगवान, क्वार्सी, रामघाट रोड,

अलीगढ़, उ.प्र. – 202001, भारत

फ़ोन : +91 - 7017993445

First Published : April 2023 - Paperback
Printed by : Thomson Press India Ltd, Repro India Ltd & Manipal Tech Ltd.
eBook by : Rajmangal ePublishers (Digital Publishing Division)

Copyright © Shivam Verma

Table of Contents

Chapter 1

How dark can it get? If someone was to ask this question tonight, the answer was around. It was a new moon night. Just like the nature of darkness, this night was also concealing secrets, and bad intents. It was concealing a heinous act that was about to happen. Why in the whole world all grimly things had to happen in night. Maybe it was a treaty between gods and demons. Maybe it was destiny of all those adverse acts.

Arvind was right there, just around the corner of the DDA Park. He knew he was being stalked. The fear of being followed by someone unknown on a new moon night was visible on his face. But was it really visible? It was late winters, but still he had that sweat on his face, that he didn't care to wipe off. No living soul was around, from whom Arvind could have asked for help. It was not just dark but a lonely night too. The question was, did he really wanted help. If so, he could have knocked on any door, but was it sensible to knock on a door and wait till someone showed up. Especially after he knew that he was being stalked, and could have been caught by the unknown danger if he stood still for any time long. Maybe he had seen it coming. Maybe he knew who was stalking him. Maybe this night has whispered the secrets in his ears.

After pacing up his steps, he found a group of trees, where he hid himself. He had known this spot from past. Arvind was deliberate while hiding and not to be spotted by the stalker. But did Arvind had any luxury of making any such assumption on such a malicious night. His heart said no, but his mind said otherwise which was tired of walking this long, and was hopeful. Arvind hid there for a while, and there were no footstep he could hear of.

Ah, maybe the danger was now gone. But the question was, on why was Arvind so scared of this stalker. Had he done some sin or some wrong with this stalker.

Then a hand came from behind that took Arvind by his collar. There they were, Arvind and the Stalker standing with faces against each other. Arvind was scared as hell, and his body was trembling with fear. But he took the courage of still seeing in the eyes of his stalker.

Arvind said, "Look, let's forget it. I am sorry for what I have done."

Arvind continued, "I cannot go back in time and change things, but still I wished I could."

Arvind said, "The man you are seeing right now, is a completely changed man. I have mend my ways."

Arvind continued, "I have a family, I have kids. Please don't do this. I know you don't want to."

Arvind said, "I will do whatever you say, but just do not kill me."

The stalker smiled, from beneath the shade of the hoodie he was wearing. He had no mercy on his face, and tonight all he sought was blood, blood of Arvind. His ruthless smile was doing the talking. Tonight this stalker was in no mood to listen anything or any justification that Arvind had to put. He had a clear agenda on his mind. He brought Arvind closer to his body and shoved a knife into his belly. That was one, with which Arvind moaned.

Then he kept shoving that knife into the belly of Arvind, again and again, till Arvind lost his last breaths. Arvind was dead, and was lying down on ground. The night of new moon had fulfilled its promise of being the dark and malicious one.

A new day had dawned, and detective Sagar Verma was reading the newspaper while sitting in his cabin in the

Akbar Nagar Police Station. The rush at the police station was all usual. There were people coming in and people going out, some with a pleasing smile and some with the rage of being wronged in their heart. As usual Delhi had shown no sign in decrease of crimes. Jitendra Singh the assistant detective of Sagar Verma was on his way to bring coffee to his boss. Last night there was a cricket match that had kept these both up all night. Obviously both were rooting for team India, but have been disappointed by their loss. Sub Inspector Ritika who had already forecasted that Team India was going to loose, was sitting with a huge smile on her face like that of a winner, like that of someone who ran the show, just opposite to Detective Sagar.

Ritika said, "Come on what is with this grumpy face, like India never loses?"

Sagar said, "The biggest loss is when your own countrymen start to predict that you are gonna lose."

Ritika said, "Oh my. Have you seen the batting line up of Australia and in how good form they are."

Sagar said, "Does that mean our bowlers couldn't handle them."

Jitendra came in with coffee, "Careful, the coffee is too hot to handle."

Sagar said, "Is there milk in it, yeah of course, the white supremacy has to be there."

Ritika couldn't help but smile. She didn't want to hurt them both with her taunts about skills of Team India. So she took off herself to sit in her cubicle. Clearly Australia has since long enjoyed the privilege of being the best cricket team in the world. Sagar though believed that no one can dominate cricket but just a good game on that given day. He always had a firm belief in capability of Team India, even in their bad days. Ritika soon started flipping through the files that had just came in, and she saw something peculiar.

Ritika said, "Oh a British Citizen was bullied and robbed in daylight. Something we should look up guys?"

Sagar said, "Oh wasn't he good enough in batting off the bad guys."

Jitendra said, "Sorry to interrupt you both, but we have a homicide, near DDA Park. Some place we are just about to hit now. So better lets wrap up our coffee."

Crimes have always been a disease, and criminals the viruses, or the bacteria. For Sagar criminals were parasite and they belonged to only one place which was behind the bars. All these years in service to the Delhi Police, Sagar had an impeccable record of catching the bad guys with whatever it takes. He was notoriously known for taking any lengths to catch the bad guys. As per Sagar, Criminals were rouge citizens of the society, and to catch them and bring them to justice, needed another rogue officer. His theory and his beliefs have always worked for him, so nobody in the Delhi Police department has ever complained. He might have been a little reckless with criminals, but when it came to results, he was a go getter. Sagar, Jitendra, and Ritika have reached the crime scene.

Hell it was, the body of Arvind was covered in all blood. He was not in his best shape. The torn flesh, and that many wounds were all pitiful to see. The scene was all surrounded by policemen, and the area was secured.

Sagar said, "I think someone is not in a very good mood."

Ritika smiled, "That makes two of them. Just saying."

Jitendra said, "We have ID'd the victim. His name is Arvind Saxena. He lives nearby in Mohan Colony."

Sagar said, "Has his kin been notified."

Jitendra said, "Well, that is just next on agenda, meanwhile i want to show you something."

Sagar was just getting the hold of the crime scene. Apart from the body of Arvind and a feet nearby, everything was neat and tidy. There were no foot marks, nor any tire marks on the road. The killer must have done this very swiftly and cautiously without leaving any trace behind. The forensics team was on to the dead body, but Sagar feared that if they would find anything else on the victim, like some DNA or any foreign human tissue. Sagar knew most of the criminals of the south Delhi. Not that they were his friends, but knowing criminals in your jurisdiction was a proactive thing or rather a good thing for any detective.

The way this murder had happened indicated that the killer had done this meticulously, fearlessly, which was an act capable only by seasoned killers. In Sagar's jurisdiction there was no one that professional. Sagar was already curious on who this new kid was on the block. They walked up to the wall near the crime scene, boundary wall of the park. There it was written in blood, I D K.

Sagar said, "I D K, what the hell is this."

Jitendra said, "I think the killer is challenging us. Who ever it is, it is someone nasty on the block."

Sagar glanced at Jitendra, while Jitendra glanced at Sagar. They knew this look, whenever a challenge was thrown upon them. This was no normal murder investigation, now it was a murder with a riddle investigation.

News about murder has always been a hot cake for news industry, and with this IDK, it was set to break the national television. Media people from all across Delhi had surrounded the crime scene, though they were not being allowed in the actual crime spot, but then the police could not have hidden it from their prying cameras. Especially this IDK, which was boldly painted on the wall, was for now the most clicked place in entire Delhi. Some youngsters were even taking selfies with this IDK in background.

Media has dubbed this murder as IDK murder, and killer as IDK murderer. It is said, that where there is smoke, there has to be fire. Top most police officials of Delhi were already on to this murder. Sagar was getting calls from his seniors to where this investigation had reached. If Sagar was to forget his diplomacy, he would have said from 8 o clock to 9 o clock. I mean in just 1 hour what else was he supposed to do. In mid of this there was a herculean task which was more important than any police procedure that he had to wrap, that was meeting with the family of Arvind Saxena. They lived nearby, and all Sagar took was a small walk. They were sitting inside the living room.

Arvind's wife Ashima who still had wet eyes said, "Who could do this to him. What bad had he done to anyone. Arvind didn't deserved it."

Ritika said, "Ma'am we are sorry for your loss, and we will do everything in our capacity to bring justice."

Jitendra gulped the tea and said, "Was there anybody who would want to harm Arvind, any enemy, or any hater."

Ashima said, "Who will want to hurt an accountant. Everyone in his workplace loved him."

Sagar exhaled, "But still there is someone who was despised by Arvind. Someone who killed him."

Ashima said, "Detective, only a maniac would do so, and paint that IDK with his blood on wall."

Sagar couldn't help but notice two kids of Arvind. At age, when Arvind was to set them off to college, he bid them farewell. Their sad and grieved face could devastate any man on the face of this planet, and fill angst against Arvind's killer. Their family was completely broken and shattered by this loss.

Sagar didn't want to bother them by keep reminding that Arvind was dead, so for now he left the house. However it was strange that Arvind's murder spot was so close to his house. As per the report, he was returning home, and if he confronted the killer so close to his house, maybe he could have given it a run to rush to his place.

But he didn't, what could have been the reason, was the killer too strong to have caught Arvind by his tail. Maybe Arvind didn't want the killer to reach at his doorstep for family's safety. These questions were all now getting clouded in Sagar's head. The chances were that Arvind knew this killer. Sagar, Ritika and Jitendra stood near the crime scene. It was such a pity that the neighbors were now all hung up on their terrace, but no one really showed up when all this was happening. Maybe it wasn't their fault, as Arvind couldn't even get a chance to scream for help.

Sagar said, "This is clearly a crime of passion."

Jitendra said, "I agree, as no damn person would stab him multiple times, unless he had some rage."

Ritika said, "I think we also need to visit his workplace, and juggle more on his family. Murderer is sure someone Arvind knew, or even had a good relationship with, least sometime before this murder."

Sagar said, "Lets nail this son of a knife. Ah, the IDK killer."

A wise man had said that memories last longer than the time it took to create them. How true it was. No one was going to forget this IDK murder anytime soon. Mean murders like these do not happen everyday, with the killer painting the wall with victim's blood. Forensics have done their test, and it was now official that this IDK was written with Arvind's blood. It didn't took any police officer to guess that hard, but now it was all official. The dead body of Arvind had gone for autopsy.

It would take some time before they came out with their version of this heinous crime.

It was post after noon and Sagar had to attend a school program of his kid with his wife, which was now running out from his schedule. So to show a gesture of good will, he went to the school at the completion of the program to pick them up. Clearly both were upset and disappointed at this behavior. Here the culprit was Sagar himself who had a day job of catching culprits. He stood beside his car with sealed lips, while his kid Arjun, and his wife Sarika hopped inside. There was an unusual silence in the car. To break the ice, Sagar turned on the stereo of the car, which got immediately turned off by Sarika.

Sarika said, "So finally you found the time, for your own kid, that too for dropping him home, for which there are Ova, Suber, and god knows what all Taxi companies."

Sagar said, "It was work, and I couldn't have just skipped. Damn this IDK killer."

Arjun peeked in from the seat behind, "IDK killer, that is so cool, dad are you working on that case."

Sagar said, "Hey Arjun, watch it, a murder cannot be cool, someone had died."

Arjun said, "Okay, okay, but did the killer wrote that IDK with blood, really."

Sagar looked back, "Young lad, no more talking about that scumbag IDK Killer, okay."

Sarika didn't say a word, but she was upset with this behavior of Sagar. How careless Sagar was for his own family. If it would have been for once, then she wouldn't have complained. But every time Sagar had a date with his family, something important came up. This couldn't have been co incidence, it was just that Sagar prioritized work more than his family, as Sarika saw it, or as anyone close to their family would see it. The ride back home was all silent. After dropping them home, Sagar straight away took off back to the Police Station.

At this very instance and to cover up his fault, he could have least escorted them home, talked for 10 to 15 minutes about the program and then left for his work, but no, Sagar didn't had that family IQ. It was like dropping off a friend. Back in police station, everyone was hooked on to this IDK killer. The autopsy was done, and the results have came in. Sagar straight away went inside his office, where Jitendra and Ritika were having sandwiches over a news program that was showing the life of Arvind.

Sagar said, "So this is how you will juggle his family and friends, by referring to a news program."

Ritika hitched and said, "Boss the autopsy is in, and you would sure like the findings."

Jitendra said, "He was stabbed 9 times in his belly, with probably a large kitchen knife."

Ritika said, "Forensics also said, there is no foreign DNA on his body. The killer was smart."

Jitendra said, "He died due to excessive bleeding and puncture of his vital organs."

Sagar exhaled, "9 stabs, I mean what had Arvind done to this killer to deserve this."

What followed was a long silence. Everyone in the room knew that Arvind must have had some feud with this killer, but no one said so. It was obvious. Talking ill about the dead was still bad. Sagar knew that this murder was no ordinary, and had some dark secrets concealed within, but what were they. God was not going to descend down to whisper in their ears, and obviously they had to find it.

A wise man had said that whatever you do in this life, gets back to you in the same life. But what was it that Arvind had done, and what was this IDK about, what was the killer trying to convey. Why was killer even trying to say something, did he wanted to get caught. Which killer in this world would want to get caught. This killer was no exception, then why all this graffiti. Did he wanted to be popular, by doing so, or wanted an ugly truth to come on surface to this world. Anyway, he had succeeded in turning the eyeballs of this country towards this murder.

Sagar said, "The only thing which comes to my mind when I see this IDK is, I don't know."

Ritika smiled, "You sure keep a track of all the trends, detective."

Jitendra said, "Was he trying to say, that I don't know Arvind. Could it be?"

Chapter 2

'I don't know', what kind of challenge was that. Was this IDK killer trying to make fool of the investigating officers? Did really the killer didn't knew Arvind Saxena, and killed him just because they crossed paths and had a heated discussion. But could a murderer stab an unknown victim 9 times in his belly. This was out of proportion. Such a passion for an unknown person, this was certainly not adding up. Was the killer running out of words before he wrote that IDK, this could have been a possibility, like I don't know what to write with Arvind's blood. Killer sure was trying to send some message across, and Sagar was not leaving this IDK in dark.

A wise man had said, that a look in the right direction is never a straight path. Sagar, Jitendra, and Ritika were checking the phone of Sagar, which was unlocked by the IT team of Akbar Nagar Police Station. There were hell lots of messages, and some unchecked WhatsUp messages, and many calls that Sagar had made during that day, until before his murder.

Jitendra said, "I think we have a lead. Check this detective, meet you at Cozy Kitchen at 8."

Jitendra continued, "That's not it, there are pictures from that night, with Arvind drinking with this person named Rajeev Mittal, as the phone book says."

Ritika said, "So the last person to come in contact with Arvind was this Rajeev."

Sagar said, "I think we have two places to hit."

Jitendra and Ritika again looked back in the pictures to see if there was any other person that accompanied them, while Sagar said, "Come on, one is Rajeev's place and other this Cozy Kitchen."

Both smiled, while Ritika got on to her computer to dig the address of Rajeev from National Database. This was a little strange, because as per Ashima, Arvind had gone to attend some office work while he was there partying with Rajeev. Why in the hell he would lie about it. The visuals that Sagar could remember from the house of Arvind certainly had that mini bar in one corner. So hiding that he was drinking was out of question, so why did Arvind lie. There was something Arvind wanted to hide, but not necessarily that he was partying that night.

So finally a person was there on police radar who could have conspired with the killer to make Arvind hang out late that night. It was too early to make such assumptions, but anything could be possible and be considered especially in a murder investigation. Team Sagar was headed to Rajeev's address. He too didn't live very far. His house was huge, bigger than Arvind's that showed the prosperity of this new suspect. Incidentally Rajeev was at home, which Sagar was hoping, as his profile on National Database said that he was an independent stock broker. Team Sagar was sitting opposite Rajeev, while he had precognition why the police had paid him a visit.

Sagar said, "So you and Arvind were partying the night he got killed."

Rajeev hesitatingly said, "Yes, but that is not a crime, and his murder, I know nothing about it."

Sagar said, "You both seem to be good friends as the pictures from his phone suggest."

Rajeev sighed, "Ah, known him since childhood."

Sagar said, "Strange that you own a SUV, such a big car, but still you left your friend to walk back home, at such late night. Didn't you consider dropping him home."

Rajeev took a big breath, "I don't know if you will trust me, I did offered him a ride, but he refused."

Sagar stood up, and started teetering in the house office of Rajeev where they were sitting. Yes Rajeev had got made an office in his house, where he dealt with his clients and operated his trading. Meanwhile Rajeev's wife came in with tea, which brought smile to the faces of police officers, probably the first time since they entered the house. Rajeev had made a point that he did offer Arvind a ride, but there was no way to corroborate that. The only option Sagar had was to trust this guy Rajeev.

It was unfortunate for a detective like Sagar to trust a stock broker what Rajeev was, but that was the deal in this statement. Up till now Rajeev was co operating with the police, so there was no room for Sagar to suspect him, except if he was a serial liar, who knew how to make poker faces while lying. Sagar took another sip from tea, which by the way was way better than those of police station, and secretly also better than what Sarika made. Sagar was now again seated back with Rajeev.

Sagar said, "This idea of partying that night, was it yours or his."

Rajeev said, "Detective you have his phone, check it. It was he who wanted to meet me that night."

Sagar looked back at Jitendra and Ritika who passed an okay gesture without making it look obvious. Sagar said, "At the time of Arvind's death, around 12 night, where exactly were you."

Rajeev said, "I was drinking up till 2 that night, was still in Cozy Kitchen, they must have me on the CCTV."

Sagar coughed, "Thanks for the co operation Rajeev, we will be in touch again, hopefully."

Team Sagar left the house of Rajeev, while their next stop was Cozy Kitchen. The answers that Rajeev gave were satisfactory and portrayed him clean. Now only they needed to check the alibi of Rajeev. A family man like Rajeev who was doing well in his life, with a big bungalow, a big car, a boutique private firm, was very less likely to commit a murder, unless there was a huge rage from the past he had harbored. A wise man had said, when in doubt, always follow your heart, but to a place that don't make you feel heartbroken.

Team Sagar had now reached Cozy Kitchen. It was early in the day, and there was very little crowd in the club. Early drinking might not have been the norm here. They straight away went on to meet the manager, who was a young lad in his twenties, named Vijay. Sagar showed him the pictures of Rajeev and Arvind.

Vijay said, "Ah that picture is enough, as I do follow news. Was expecting police at doorstep"

Sagar said, "So do you remember anything unusual, that happened on the unfortunate night."

Vijay said, "Nothing out of the blue, in fact I was the person who got them apply a coupon from internet, which was being unable to be redeemed by one of my waiters, as it has expired. We do not want bad customer experiences on our menu, so I agreed for redemption of the coupon. That was first when they caught my attention."

Sagar said, "Okay, so did Arvind had any argument with his friend or anyone else in club."

Vijay said, "Nothing. Both were enjoying like old pals meeting after ages."

While they were having the conversation, the waiter who wasn't able to redeem the coupon had joined, and he told the same story to Team Sagar. Apparently there was nothing suspicious unless the people at Cozy Kitchen had done rehearsals of their statements before hand. With seeing the interiors and the gentry one could have easily guessed that this club was very up market, not the kind of place middle class man like Arvind would hang out, but sure like a place where Rajeev would. Sagar was right about it, as the waiter also got the bill record of that night where it was clearly mentioned that the bill was checked out by Rajeev and not Arvind. Well that was understandable.

Sagar was now looking at the cameras that were installed at the place. They were quite in number, and just like what CCTV does, they must have captured everything from that night.

Sagar said, "Was there anybody else that was keeping an eye on them, or had followed them in this club."

Vijay tried thinking, along with the waiter, and they said unanimously, "Nobody, I am sure."

Sagar said, "Mr. Rajeev says he was in the club till 2, anybody to corroborate that."

Vijay said, "Of course sir, he is our regular, and he sure was till 2, at the time when we close. The reason why I remember it so clearly"

Sagar smiled, "Okay, now we will be needing CCTV footage from that night, all of it."

Sagar had no such reasons to trust everything that Vijay said, because there was a CCTV for it. Vijay didn't hesitated even a bit in giving the footage, though normally an aware manager would need permission from court. To top it he even showed the surveillance video from that night to Sagar from a birds eye on the systems of the club. Everything was looking intact. No prying eyes. Each person on the floor that night was enjoying the moment like if it was their last.

How ironic it was that one of them, Arvind Saxena was really living his last night.

Jitendra took the CCTV for detailed examination, while they left. A wise man had said, you will find everything you want, only if you are ready to give everything it needs. Talking of Sagar, he actually lived on these words. They were headed to Arvind's house, assuming that family had enough time to grief over the dead, and now would talk like normal people do. The truth was that no time in this world was enough to get over the death of a family member, but still they must now have been in a good mental shape to help out Sagar. Team Sagar was sitting opposite Ashima, and Arvind's parents.

Sagar said, "I know it's a hard time, but we have some questions."

Ashima said, "Oh Please, we are just getting used to hard times. What is it?"

Sagar looked back at Jitendra and Ritika, while he continued, "We have a suspect, though he didn't commit the murder as his alibi is solid, but we are still looking into him. Do you know anyone named Rajeev Mittal."

Ashima took a deep breath, "That dog, of course we know him. He had almost ruined our lives once."

Sagar gulped, "Okay, and how so."

Ashima said, "You must have known by now, that Rajeev is a stock broker. He was my husband's friend from long, since they were kids. My husband trusted him. When Rajeev had opened his new business, this stock broking one, he somehow tricked my husband to sell one of our property and invest in some company. Like I had feared and had even warned my husband, the company crashed. At that time our household was in worst financial crisis, as my husband had also invested all of our savings. That crook was no good for us.

I mean what friend does that. Wait, I will show it you, if you don't believe."

Before Sagar could stop Ashima, and say that he totally believed in her just like his atheist mind believed that were no gods, she left. His detective instincts told him, why not see something solid as a proof which could also be used later to build up a court case. Now the picture of the relationship between Rajeev and Arvind was coming out from silhouette. For Rajeev, Arvind was a fat pig whom he had butchered once, and maybe was again going to butcher him. All those friendly vibes existed just because Rajeev could get to be the stock broker for Arvind. This was nowhere near to be called friendship. This was a cynical relationship where Arvind had high hopes from a friend, while Rajeev only cared about the business he brought.

In all of this, Sagar was little baffled, on where did Arvind had this deal of money to invest in stocks. As per the condition of household, Arvind was merely a middle class man who met his ends through his salary. Would he again chose to invest in stocks that too through Rajeev. Sagar couldn't comprehend this situation and the equation between those two. Meanwhile Ashima returned with a file of papers. There was little anger in her eyes, which she tried her best not showing it to team Sagar, but then her emotions were too strong to stay hidden.

Ashima said, "Look at these, these are proofs of the stock dealing. My brother also deals in finance, he told Arvind that this company was a shell company, and we should sue Rajeev. But oh, that great old friendship came in between. That Rajeev is nothing else than a back biting snake."

Sagar flipped through the pages. Apparently Arvind bought shares worth 100 Rs, which tanked to 5 Rs, in just two months. This was a scam, and he should have forwarded this to the financial fraud division of Police. But this case was old and chances were slim. Sagar said, "Was there any chance that Arvind wanted to invest again."

Ashima said, "Only if that Rajeev tricked him in doing so."

Sagar said, "Did Arvind had that deal of money to invest, or maybe he had already invested, and was in some sort of debt to Rajeev or maybe someone else. I hope you are getting at it."

Ashima waved her head, "The only good thing about my husband in this, he would never borrow money."

Sagar nodded, "Thanks for sharing this information. We will meet again till I have something."

This meeting of two old pals had pinched Ashima, that Arvind was again seeing Rajeev. This was the part that Sagar hated the most about his job, sharing uncomfortable facts with family of victim. The information that Team Sagar had got in lieu was pretty useful. In a nutshell the status quo was that Arvind would never borrow money, and if he had invested in stocks, from some of his savings or other financial instruments, his family would have got to know about it. So if he was willing to invest in stocks, where would Arvind get this money from. Neither Arvind had won some lottery, nor had he the budget.

Rounding back to the suspect, Rajeev might have been a fraud but murderer, no. He would have other ideas of butchering this family man. Rajeev was not the IDK killer, neither did he had balls to kill someone. But what if Arvind had already invested in stocks, and Rajeev was not telling it. Sagar didn't want to rule out this possibility as he thought, while he sat with Jitendra and Ritika.

A wise man had said, Money is the root cause of all troubles, whether you have it or not. In here money could have been the problem. Sagar took a sip of coffee that he had on his table.

Sagar said, "What if Arvind had already invested in stocks, while Rajeev didn't wanted to pay him back, so Rajeev got him murdered. Could it be possible?"

Jitendra said, "But who would Rajeev hire, maybe a hit man, or local mob."

Ritika said, "But this style of killing is way above their passion and certainly not their cup of tea."

Sagar said, "I know, I know, but let's give it a check."

Jitendra said, "Okay, I will get Rajeev's phone records and tap his phone too. Hope he has something in history, or spills the truth out to someone."

Sagar nodded while he left the day as dusted. Today Arjun didn't had school because of a public holiday, and Sagar had promised him that they will have dinner together. Well that wasn't the catch, the catch was that Sagar had agreed that he will bring pizza for dinner, or get it delivered. There were very few moments where Sagar actually spent time with his family. Sarika always complained, but Sagar never acted like the policeman he was with his family, so the complaints went unanswered. Sarika was so fed up with round the clock job of Sagar that she had actually stopped complaining about it. Arjun who was just a kid only considered his dad as a hero. What else could kids think of their dad?

A wise man had said, that family is what not we get, but what we give to. Clearly these words were not very ideal for Sagar. The family was seated at the table, while Sagar was checking his phone, Arjun was checking the pizzas, actually he had already started eating, while Sarika watched them. There were two kids in the house that didn't care about the concept of family time. Sagar noticed and got back to the table.

Sagar said, "So champ how is it going in school."

Arjun had just taken a big bite and with stuffed mouth said, "Everything is cool dad, I am getting good grades."

Sagar said, "You know that is the reason why I have also got ordered ice cream too."

Sarika slowly slipped in, "But that might not be forever, he needs more time as he grows."

Sagar said, "We have already talked about it. Give it some time and we will see."

Sarika snapped back, "No, we have talked about it. He needs to be in a boarding school, because as he grows up, his studies are going to get tough, and more demanding. And by the way, even I have a day job."

Sagar slowly left the table with a box of pizza and took a seat at the couch which was not so far from the dining table. He was still in the room, but away from being bombarded by provoking questions. A pretext would be, that Sarika had been insisting that Arjun be sent to Boarding School, so he could concentrate on his studies, and Sarika got some time to focus on her career. But Sagar was little reluctant, as he wanted Arjun to enjoy his childhood, and make memories for ever. In boarding school his personal life would be so dead. This was a bitter face off that Sagar avoided with his wife. Meanwhile Jitendra's call dropped on his cell phone.

Jitendra said, "You were right detective. He had borrowed money. We got a lead."

Chapter 3

All that starts well, ends well. Sagar was now seeing the relevance of these word in this case, on this day. Just like good mornings he had, the night was ending with a good news, a lead in IDK murder. But was this night going to end with just a good news, no. Sagar was already in his bedroom getting ready to head out. Arjun the slow eater was still enjoying the pizza, and Sarika was fuming out of words. She couldn't decide if she should yell at Sagar, or should she just ignore pretending that she was not with him on this. Whoever had said that the life of a policeman is so exciting, should also meet their families to only know that all the excitement is in the job but none at home.

Sagar was now out in his car, driving straight to Arvind's house. This was where Jitendra and Ritika were. A wise man had said that the only things you find are the ones who are also finding you. Sagar stood outside Arvind's house. Apparently a huge crowd had also gathered. Sagar was not sure what was actually happening behind the scenes. He spotted Jitendra like an old lost brother to get a hang of the situation.

Jitendra said, "There is a loan shark, Amit Desai, who claims that Arvind had borrowed 30 lacs from him."

Sagar said, "That is a lot of money. Does he has any proof of it."

Ritika barged in, "Yes a signed deed, which confirms that Arvind took the money on day of his murder."

Sagar sighed, "So what did he now put as security."

Ritika said, "Some fixed Deposits, and his PF account."

Sagar said, "Could this man Amit Desai, be the killer."

Jitendra shrugged and so did Ritika. Now inside the house there was a whole heated discussion going on. This man Amit, wanted his money back, which would require Ashima's signature on some papers. While Ashima was arguing, if his husband has taken the money where was it. Both were strongly holding their guards. Now apart from a murderer there was another 30 lacs which no one knew where they were. There was already the pain of seeing Arvind die, and now his family also had to also bear this another shock loss of 30 lacs. Sometimes god throws us situation where he himself would feel sorry about it.

It was Ashima who had called the police claiming that Amit was trying to scare the family to give the money. It was very normal for loan sharks to use this tactic. But as Arvind was dead, this had to get here, to the Detective of Akbar Nagar Police Station. Sagar entered the house and tried calming down Ashima. He got them all seated.

Amit said, "I don't care if Arvind is dead, I just want my money back."

Ashima said, "What money he is talking about. I am sure he never gave any money to Arvind, and now he is dead so he wants to fish on our family."

Amit said, "Listen, this deed is signed by your husband, this is a living proof that he took the money."

Sagar barged in, "Where were you at the time of Arvind's murder, 12 that night."

Amit hopelessly swayed his head, "Can't believe it is getting there. Anyways, I was in my home watching a movie, and my wife, my children, my servant, my driver, they can corroborate on that."

It was Sagar's job to suspect him, as he was no saint, he was a loan shark, who are infamous for committing crimes. Jitendra had even pulled the records of this man, and it seemed that in past he was involved in 14 different court cases, though never convicted. That was the biggest catch. Either he was too smart to get through the loopholes of Indian Judiciary system, or he really was a clean man getting caught up in muddy waters again and again because of his profession.

The point was that Amit was a smart person, who would never disturb a family entangled in a murder investigation if he hadn't given the money. It was too messy to get involved with Detectives, least he must have known this through his previous 14 cases. So if this man Amit was telling the truth, then Arvind must have met Rajeev to invest again in stocks. But if that was the case, then why didn't Rajeev tell detectives about it. Something was very fishy over here, and Sagar could smell it separately from the coffee that maid of the house had prepared and served. Sagar got back again to Amit.

Sagar said, "What is the proof that you gave him money."

Amit smiled, "I knew it would get there, so I have saved it for police. See I have CCTV covering my office which is in my home, and the entry gate of my house. See for yourself."

Amit opened his phone which was connected to the CCTV footage of his house stored on cloud, and showed Arvind taking a bag of cash. He even opened it to count the cash, which was all there in the camera, and then Arvind leaving the house with the same bag to the street. Amit was telling the truth, and he had proof of it. Now a bigger question came in to the mind of Sagar. Was it because of the money that Arvind got killed. But when he was walking back home he had no bag. In fact when he entered the Cozy Kitchen, even then he didn't had any bag. So where did this bag disappeared.

Arvind had exited the house of Amit late in evening, then he entered the Cozy Kitchen after 2 hours, without any bag. So this money went missing somewhere in those 2 hours. Maybe Arvind gave it to someone to keep it safe, because he didn't wanted to come back home with all that cash and an explanation to give to his wife. Whatever it was, finding of this bag was now important for Arvind as it might also reveal the identity of killer. Meanwhile Ashima was losing her cool.

Ashima yelled, "But we don't have that money, so we are giving back nothing."

Amit also yelled, "I will drag you to court, as I am just filing this complaint."

Sagar intervened, "Hey easy, easy. Give us couple of days, before we find those 30 lacs of yours."

Amit rushed out, while Ashima held her head, "How am I supposed to give 30 lacs to him."

Sagar said, "Don't worry we will find that money which you can throw on his face."

Outside police had dispersed the crowd that had gathered. Seriously IDK also have 3 characters, while the money which was missing from here was also 30 lacs, could this be the reason why the killer wrote that IDK on the wall. It was all just a theory which Sagar was spinning in his head. But what if it was true and this all was about money. It would have been stupid of a detective to ignore such a possibility. Now the question was where did this money go. Jitendra had got the IT team sit on the mobile phone of Arvind to track his location in those 2 hours. This was the best shot that they have got.

Sagar, Ritika and Jitendra sat in his cabin checking the CCTV footage around the area where Amit lived, in hopes they could find a trail of Arvind and track where did he dumped the bag. It has been 3 to 4 hours, checking different CCTV cameras, but still there was no clue. The metro station CCTV cameras were the first ones they checked, but Arvind was nowhere. Probably he must have taken a cab or auto rickshaw to the Cozy Kitchen. He probably must have also stopped at somewhere in between to give the bag to someone, but who could be that person whom Arvind trusted with 30 lacs that he borrowed and were not even his earnings.

Sagar said, "Why would Arvind give a bag of 30 lacs to someone, just because to hide it from his wife."

Jitendra said, "It makes sense, as his wife is sure a trouble maker, as we saw it."

Sagar said, "Why not just give it to Rajeev, as anyway it was going to land there."

Ritika said, "Maybe because Arvind didn't wanted to show all his cards to Rajeev."

Sagar said, "As he had gotten cheated once. Maybe he was testing Rajeev by meeting him at Cozy Kitchen."

A wise man had said, that a theory is not what you believe, but what you want to believe. Sagar didn't want to leave any stone unturned. Meanwhile the IT team had marked the route that Arvind took from Amit's house to Cozy Kitchen. The revelation came as quite a surprise to Team Sagar, as it was a direct route from Amit's house to Cozy Kitchen. The movement of Arvind that day however indicated two stops in between that too of 5 minutes each. It could have been the stops where Arvind used the time to give that bag to someone else.

The police team at Akbar Nagar Police Station had also reviewed the CCTV footage of those two areas, but they were unable to find even one thing about that bag drop off. Now this bag was becoming like a big mystery for Team Sagar, bigger than that bold IDK on the wall. For the death of Arvind, they at least have got the dead body, but this bag had like vanished into a thin air with no clue on who took it. A task force was created, by Sagar who would now go to these two areas to check if they had seen Arvind dealing, talking, or meeting with someone. This was the best move Sagar could have thought of.

Sagar said, "Meet everyone you can, juggle every street side vendor, show them the picture of Arvind, and make sure that they remember something from that day."

Jitendra said, "As you command sir, we will leave nothing untouched."

Ritika said, "Let us hope we find a clue."

Sagar said, "This is not about hope, this is our only shot, and we got to make best use of it."

Sagar said, "And Ritika you are not going with Jitendra, you got to catch up with auto unions, and taxi unions to see if someone from them picked Arvind up that day."

This IDK killer was going nowhere exotic with this killing, nor was this person who took off 30 lacs from Arvind, in case if they were two different people. A wise man had said that what you seek for, is what you want to get and not what you deserve to get. In here, the efforts were all up, and maybe Team Sagar deserved more than what they had got or maybe less. Jitendra was going from one street vendor to other, but no one had spotted Arvind. Everyone just had one word to say, nothing on this man. There was no one who recognized Arvind from that picture, except ones that have seen him on news.

Jitendra even thought that might be the driver of that taxi or auto might have taken these few minutes for himself and not for Arvind. Meanwhile the taxi unions and Cab unions have circulated the picture of Arvind in their internal

WhatsUp group. Wait, there was a match coming up, as one of the taxi driver recognized Arvind. Finally the great hard work was getting paid off. Team Sagar, except Jitendra was on their way to meet this Taxi driver. Sagar was already excited about this fateful and hard worked lead. Soon they stood facing each other.

Sagar said, "So you recognize this man from other day."

Taxi Driver said, "Yes Detective. His name was Arvind, he even told me that."

Sagar said, "Was he carrying a bag that day."

Taxi Driver exhaled, "I knew there was something wrong. I am sure that bag had stash of money in it. I mean the way he was carrying that bag close to his chest had revealed everything. I didn't say a word, because it was none of my business, but still I had my doubts. Yes he carried the bag all along till the time I dropped him off at Cozy Kitchen."

Sagar was baffled, "So when he took off from your Taxi at Cozy Kitchen he still had that bag."

Taxi driver nodded, "Positive Detective. He still had that bag."

OMFG, it was the only word that came to Sagar's head, and not that IDK. So apparently this exchange of bag took place outside the gates of Cozy Kitchen, because Arvind didn't got that bag inside the club. Now the bells have started to ring in the head of Sagar, but he didn't say a word. Instead he took the taxi driver, to the place where exactly he dropped off Arvind. See this club Cozy Kitchen had two gates, so Sagar needed to be sure. Now they were moving along with the taxi driver to that exact spot.

A wise man had said, that it is not criminal the problem, but the real problem was crime. Till the last moment in this earth there was crime, there will be criminals. Sagar hadn't said it but deep inside he knew which gate the taxi driver was going to stop. Yes there was already a theory spinning and brewing in his head. He couldn't stop to find out what the truth was. The taxi driver stopped at the gate number 2 of Cozy Kitchen. Sagar immediately smiled and looked around if there were any CCTV cameras. But alas there were none, but it didn't stopped Sagar from hoping that he could have a lead from here. Soon he spotted a homeless man on the pavement of the road. As per Sagar's clear memory this homeless man was there even on the first time they had visited the place. Sagar approached him.

Sagar said, "Hey why don't I buy you lunch, dinner, and give you some money. But for that you need to juggle your memory and tell me if you have seen this man."

Sagar showed him his cell phone with picture of Arvind, "Yes I saw him couple of days ago. He looked suspicious."

Ritika smiled, "Why did he looked suspicious to you."

Homeless man said, "He had this bag close to his chest, which he gave it to another man. It had cash right."

Sagar showed him a picture and said, "Did that man gave the bag to this man."

Homeless man said, "Yes that was him, but how do you know that."

Sagar had that winning smile on his face. It felt that he had won half the battle. By the way this picture was of Rajeev Mittal. Yes it was that son of a bag lying dog, that took 30 lacs of cash from Arvind on that night. Sagar was feeling happy inside that it was another closed case. The IDK killer or Rajeev Mittal was after all not that smart. But in this whole theory of Sagar there was a mismatch, which was that Rajeev had a strong alibi at the time of murder, but then 30 lacs was a great amount to hire a hit man to do this job. That was the best explanation that Sagar came close to.

They were on their way to the house of Rajeev, while that homeless man had been brought to the Akbar Nagar Police Station to be groomed up to give up an official statement. The fate of Rajeev was now sealed and all that was left was a confession or admittance of crime from Rajeev himself. Wife of Arvind, Ashima was right that Rajeev was certainly a snake, or rather a greedy snake who would even bite his own friend for money. What a shame it was in the world of friends that people like Rajeev also existed. Team Sagar was sitting in front of Rajeev, who was little worried to police drop by again.

Sagar said, "So now you are richer by 30 lacs, am I right Rajeev."

Rajeev stuttered, "Huh, sorry. I am not getting what you are saying detective."

Sagar said, "We have an eye witness who saw you taking that bag from Arvind. Now come on spill it up, unless you want to face the fury of the prosecutor in court."

Rajeev said, "You are lying, isn't it. You are just playing with facts, but you cannot fool me."

Sagar said, "Of course we cannot fool you because you are too smart for it, like obviously you have two felonies to your name. One frauding Arvind of 30 lacs and other killing him in cold blood.. Anyways, I wish you best of luck, while we see you in court."

Rajeev held his head, "Wait, I took that bag of 30 lacs from him. But I didn't killed him. I swear."

That was the moment which Sagar had been waiting for. The confession came right out. Sagar was sure about the part of 30 lacs, but was little dubious about the IDK murder. Rajeev made his beliefs a little more strong. Sagar might have not said it, but the seeds of suspicion were already sown. There they were, the kids and wife of Rajeev, but Sagar had no pity for them, as that place was reserved for Arvind's family in this investigation.

Rajeev said, "I had no intention of keeping those 30 lacs, but only to invest on behalf of Arvind. But then on that morning I heard about his death, it was then I made my mind to conceal that fact as no one would know. Trust me, I never put even a scratch on Arvind."

Sagar relentlessly said, "You are under arrest Rajeev for a fraud of 30 lacs."

Chapter 4

A wise man had said that all criminals of this world get caught because of one mistake, the one being a criminal. Rajeev who pretended to be a friend of Arvind was now facing fraud charges, and he was not getting out of it as easily as he had got himself in. All eyes were on him. To create public pressure, Sagar had even given statements to some of the leading news papers and media houses. The news had spread like wild fire, and many were already holding Rajeev responsible for IDK killing. For them the equation was simple that Rajeev did this for greed of those 30 lacs. But Sagar as a detective had to get some proof in given circumstances of a solid alibi.

It was cases like these that made Detective Sagar happy that he didn't had many friends. What was the point of having a back biting friend. Not necessarily all friends were like Rajeev, but in the world we live the chances were high that they would have done something similar in a situation like this. Certainly the world was moving in a very poignant direction, but that was all together another debate. What mattered was that team Sagar was moving inside the cell Rajeev was held. It was confrontation time.

Sagar said, "Rajeev this is your first and last chance, admit that you killed Arvind, and I will ensure that Judge goes lenient on you. You can trust me on that."

Rajeev said, "Why don't you understand, I didn't killed him. I was in Cozy Kitchen."

Jitendra said, "I got this detective. Okay let us rephrase, that you ordered the hit on Arvind. Admit that."

Rajeev said, "The thing is that I just got a little greedy. That is all. I acted like an opportunist."

Ritika said, "You are not getting it Rajeev. If we find that you got Arvind killed a hard way, then that is going to fall on you even harder. So why not let's just save ourselves some time."

Rajeev said, "I know this good cop and bad cop thing, and I also know that you have no proof against me for killing Arvind."

Rajeev might have been the killer, or maybe he wasn't, this was uncertain, but he was certainly not that stupid. The reason police was still talking to him was because they didn't had any evidences against him. The great punch line of law applied here, innocent until proven guilty. It was true, and it also was true, that if Rajeev didn't confessed to this crime, he would only be charged with fraud. This didn't brought joy in his heart, but deep inside Rajeev was feeling a little secure that least he would not have to spend the rest of his life in prison for murder.

This was not it, he was also regretting the very morning when he woke up to hear that news which played tricks in his mind to actually keep those 30 lacs. Sometimes devil plays with you without even letting you know. Rajeev must have thought that these 30 lacs will disappear into thin air considering police will be engrossed in Arvind's murder investigation. Not even in his dreams he had imagined that he would be praying to his gods for being acquitted from a prison cell. These obnoxious dreams only occur to criminals when in prison cell. But wait, Team Sagar had not yet given up. There was a still lot of talking left to do with Rajeev. Sagar made a move.

Sagar said, "Okay, so you think that you will only get prison time for the fraud you did. But what if before that sentence comes down I do a little chat with the judge and he sentences you equally like of a murder."

Jitendra said, "That is not it, what if I hand down this murder investigation to some of my juniors who are good at cooking cases even the wrong way."

Ritika said, "What if we tell another of your prison mate, to give you some good welcome."

Jitendra said, "Or rather your ticket way up."

Sagar said, "A lot can happen Rajeev. Now it all depends on you, about what you want to happen."

Rajeev broke down, "Do whatever you feel like, but I am not confessing to a crime I didn't commit."

Team Sagar exchanged a glance, while they could see the wet eyes of Rajeev. Being in prison must sure be depressing. These wet eyes were both because Rajeev was in such a miserable situation and also because of guilt he had of using a friends death for his own advantage. Team Sagar went out of the interrogation room leaving Rajeev with his troubled thoughts and the proposal they had offered him. Deep down Sagar had suddenly started to get a gut feeling that Rajeev was not the person behind this IDK murder and it was not because of his poignant drama.

Rajeev was really an opportunist that is all. No matter how close friend Arvind might have considered him, but deep inside Rajeev just wanted to take advantage of Arvind. It was stupid of Arvind to have trusted Rajeev blindly despite of the betrayal in past. Wait, calling a dead person stupid was a disgrace. He was better off resting in peace. A wise man had said, dig the dead and you will have another grave empty. Rajeev might have been a man with low morals but he definitely didn't had the stomach of killing another man. The bigger mess was already outside, as media had already started labeling him the IDK killer. But honestly who cared what media thought. They will always have hundred of stories around same person. What mattered was the people who were now expecting that Police punished this merciless IDK killer. Meanwhile in Sagar's cabin over cup of coffee.

Sagar said, "My gut says that IDK killer is still out."

Jitendra said, "With all due respect detective, this man Rajeev had already fooled us once, by not telling the truth, and my gut says that he is trying to fool us again by not admitting to the murder of Arvind."

Ritika said, "My stand point is in kind of middle. Rajeev looks innocent, but his acts says otherwise."

Jitendra said, "All rich people look innocent, just saying."

Sagar said, "You know Rajeev had got the best lawyer on board, who must have sure suggested that Rajeev was about to return the money, when all this happened, or was about to invest in stocks as Arvind wanted him to and hand over the papers to his wife. But still this man is confessing and maintaining his ground."

Sagar continued, "If I consider this, then his hit man the IDK killer is smarter than him, for having left no trace."

Sagar had a valid point, and he had an unwavering faith that the lawyer was going to use it in the court. Sagar had seen such cases day in day out, and there was no big deal in assuming so. But what would make this case trickier was the death of Arvind. It was not just any death, it was a merciless killing with a knife, where after the killer wrote that IDK on the wall with blood. Wait, in mid of all this that IDK in blood was losing its due attention, the big IDK in blood. This IDK got to have bigger significance in this murder. Why would a murderer risk waiting all this time to extract blood from the body of Arvind and then go on to take the pain of painting IDK on the wall. The full form of IDK might have been I don't know, but clearly the killer was trying to send across some message. With the confidence of this message, the murderer must be doing the right thing in his conscious. He actually might have justified that murder with this IDK. Psycho killers are all the same. He was right in his place and wanted the world to know this. IDK was not just some fun graffiti, but a bold statement of being right. Ashima had dropped in the office of Sagar.

Ashima said, "I knew that dog was no good to us, but how could he kill his own friend."

Sagar said, "Ashima we are doing our best, but what we have as of now, doesn't indicate that this cheater Rajeev killed your husband. We fear the killer might still be at large."

Ashima said, "He is not the killer, because you don't have proof, or is he really not the killer."

Sagar nodded, "Well, actually both."

Ashima said, "Detective you got to find this killer, because I want to see him or her in the eyes and ask what wrong did my husband do, for deserving such a brutal departure."

Sagar said, "I promise, that you will get that chance. Now Jitendra will take your statement regarding these 30 lacs"

A promise to a widow about her dead husband's killer was the last thing a policeman should make. Sagar had already known that this IDK killer was damn smart, and in present circumstances the police was still clueless. Police was just beating around the bush. A wise man had said, that all acts of the men who want to make a difference leave their marks behind. Sagar had lived by these words all his life, and was sure that this IDK killer was also trying to leave his mark behind, like a cult. It was wrong to assume that IDK was only mocking police, but it was for the people to judge. Was IDK the only thing that he had and he wanted to leave behind. IDK was the simplest abbreviation that anyone could have used.

A non tech savvy guy like Sagar also had not to guess that hard that it stood for I don't Know, but what if this IDK had two meanings. It was possible, because a challenge like cracking the code of IDK couldn't have been that simple. There has to be a catch. Well that was it, IDK had two meanings. But what could have been the second meaning. Team Sagar was sitting in Sagar's office while Sagar took the lead.

Sagar said, "I am sure that this IDK killer has given us a challenge. I am sure that this IDK, which means I don't Know also has another meaning. Yep this killer wants to play with us."

Jitendra said, "But what could be the other meaning of IDK. I mean like that we wont find anything."

Sagar clichéd, "Well maybe it is from the past, some injustice did in another investigation."

Ritika said, "In that case Arvind had to be a part of it, but I have double checked. This Arvind guy had no connection to any criminal cases in past. Forget Criminal, he doesn't even has a traffic ticket to his name."

Sagar said, "Name, well, that could be it. Maybe IDK is a short form of a name."

Team Sagar glanced at each other, while Ritika said, "Sure boss we will get on it."

There it was, maybe IDK meant a name, a name which could lead the police to the killer. Maybe IDK was the name of the killer himself. Sagar damned himself on why didn't he thought about this at the first place. It made perfect sense, as IDK could also have been a nick name of somebody following his initials and last name. Maybe this IDK name was the reason why this IDK killer, killed Arvind. The broken pieces have now started to make some sense.

Meanwhile the real police work had got into action. Ritika along with Jitendra was already on the National Database, searching people whose name would sum down to IDK and lived in Delhi NCR. Well this was an assumption that the IDK killer was from Delhi. This assumption was also made because Arvind was born and brought up in Delhi. So assuming that the killer knew Arvind, he had to be from Delhi. There were lots of assumptions, but the police work was a synonym to making assumptions. A huge list came down by the result and it was practically impossible to narrow it down.

Sagar said, "Let us filter this list, with people who have lived in the radius of 5 km, from the house of Arvind. Remember it is not necessary that they live now in that circle, as they could have lived there in past too."

Jitendra said, "You mean the killer was a neighbor of Arvind."

Sagar said, "I am saying that because the killer definitely knew the neighborhood which gave him confidence enough to kill Arvind in the vicinity of his own house."

Ritika said, "But what if this IDK name is not of killer, but a link to killer."

Sagar said, "Let us just stick to the plan, rest we will figure later."

Ritika and Jitendra got on to work. The filter suggestion from Sagar had certainly made their work easier. Finding a name IDK in 5 km of radius was much better than finding the names from entire Delhi NCR. The radius could have been much less, but Sagar took it into consideration that this person might have changed places in past. This was all just but his gut feeling and summation of all these years of policing experience. A wise man had said, if you can learn to trust your gut, you will need lesser people to advise you.

Sagar was just hoping that they could get on a lead. If it was true that this IDK killer had left this IDK as a challenge to the Police, then Sagar assumed that he must have done it so deliberately to follow the working style of police. Eventually what was the point of leaving clues if they do not get cracked. Sagar was just hoping that this IDK better had two meanings, or they would again be caught up in void. The biggest worry was, what if this killer was trying to confuse the police with whatsoever no meaning behind that IDK. Sagar just hoped for the best. Ritika and Jitendra came back with a smile on their face.

Jitendra said, "Boss I think you got it right, we do have a match."

Sagar exhaled, "I have never wanted to listen anything that much from you. What's the lead?"

Ritika said, "Well for starters, he is a media man, associated with Daily Herald."

Sagar said, "Then how is he connected to Arvind."

Ritika said, "Well, I do not know about the connection, but this man certainly used to live in the same locality where Arvind lives. And I am pretty sure that he knows Arvind too."

Sagar smiled, "Then we better go and check him."

So now this man the media man, was Ishwar Das Kashyap. The IDK maybe meant talking about this Ishwar Das Kashyap. Team Sagar had their big lead, but still with ambiguity of this lead being genuine or just a shot in the dark was based on hunches. The only established fact with this lead was that Ishwar was once a neighbor Arvind, so sure must have some connection with him. You know things like coincidence rarely existed in Police Work.

A wise man had said, that sign of a good cop is that he doesn't believes in coincidences. Many great people of this world have tagged probability of coincidences to human connections. Coincidences were now science. Anyways, this was a topic to debated some place else but not here and not now. Team Sagar was headed to the address of this IDK. Sagar was hoping hard that they hit some connection between these two. If Sagar was right, then this killer must have known both Ishwar and Arvind, also the connection between them. The profession of this Ishwar being a media man was a rather odd connection to a normal common man like Arvind. Maybe this Ishwar had done some story on Arvind, but about what. Arvind was not a celebrity, nor a politician, nor some intellectual property on the block. The answers to these questions were now with Ishwar. Team Sagar was sitting with Ishwar at his residence.

Sagar said, "Thank you Ishwar, for talking to us. Being a media man, you must have heard about the IDK killing. I am sure, that you must have read some pieces on it."

Ishwar said, "Of course I have heard about it. But how can I help in this."

Sagar said, "As per our intel, you used to live in the same locality where Arvind did, the victim of this IDK killer."

Ishwar surprisingly said, "Okay, so what are you suggesting Detective."

Sagar said, "Don't get me wrong. But all I am suggesting is that you used to share neighborhood with him. I am sure you knew him maybe from the past."

Ishwar said, "Detective I have only lived in that locality briefly. I know many people from the neighborhood, but I don't recall knowing Arvind. In fact I also don't recall doing any stories on Arvind. Believe me my memory had never failed me, if that is what you are doubtful about. But wait, in case I am missing something, I have something for you that might be of help."

Was all this matchup of IDK was in vain. Sagar thought maybe this man was telling the truth. He had no other reason to lie. He was a middle aged man by appearance and little older than by age. The last act he would do was murder Arvind and write that IDK on the wall with his trembling hands. God, this IDK killer was now becoming pain in the back of Sagar. How smart could a man be to leave no trace. How smart could a man be to keep a murder revelation away from the police and keep them guessing. Meanwhile Ishwar got back from his bedroom carrying a huge folder. Now what was that, team Sagar was already curious about it.

Ishwar said, "This folder has all the stories I have been part of. I don't recall Arvind being part of them, but sure you can help yourselves Detective."

Sagar smiled while he took the folder from Ishwar. This was really a nice gesture from this old man. Then his phone rang. Sagar picked it while a police officer said, "Detective, the IDK killer has struck again."

Chapter 5

IDK Killer strikes again. It was all over the National News, it was all over the social media, and it had become a hot topic of discussion just within an hour. Sagar hadn't anticipated it, but it did happen quicker than it should. A wise man had said that if you want to live your life on edge, pray all your nightmares come true. This killing was like another nightmare for Delhi Police. With the public pressure of Arvind's death, this murder was surely going to hot up the war rooms of Delhi Police. Sagar was already on his way to examine the crime scene, and was occupied thinking about IDK Killer. This was a game for this killer. Before Sagar could dig deeper into the murder of Arvind, he had struck again. Was this a start of something nefarious, or the end of some angst? Only time could tell.

Meanwhile in Sagar's car, Jitendra was already lauding the balls that this IDK killer had. With one open investigation in his name, he had committed another murder. Wasn't he afraid of the Police, or the law and order system of the country? Was he that confident that police would never be able to nab him. Whatever the reason might be, there was another man lying dead near a renowned club. Team Sagar were standing facing the dead body, while other Police Officers briefed him.

Sagar said, "So who is he, any ID on him."

Police Officer said, "Yes, he had his wallet intact in his jeans. His name is Shah Faisal."

Sagar said, "The same Modus Operandi. This is sure done by our IDK Killer."

Jitendra said, "Who called it in."

Police Officer said, "The housekeeper of the club, who came out to throw the trash."

Sagar said, "Any witnesses, or did anybody saw something."

The police officer shook his head. Sagar knew that this IDK killer was too smart to leave any clues behind. Leaving no clues behind was also a part of his modus operandi. Now even Sagar was having second thoughts about this killer having the balls. The dead body of Faisal laid there in cold blood, with repetitive knife stab marks in his belly. This IDK killer was merciless. The fury or passion with which these victims were killed was a high indicator that this IDK killer knew them both, or maybe he was just a psycho. Whatever mental status he might have, this case now had became of high importance. It was now on Sagar to catch this killer to keep the city safe.

2 dead bodies in a week, and if this killer was psycho he would not stop, which would mean many more dead bodies and a PR disaster for Delhi Police. After a long Sagar had came across such a sturdy killer. Now the most intriguing part of the crime scene, was somewhere the police officer was leading the Team Sagar to. Soon they stood against it. Sagar was already feeling disgusted to see it. While Jitendra got a picture of it clicked. As per the last investigation, the handwriting was a perfect match. They stood there gazing the other clue.

Sagar said, "BUT. But, now what does that means."

Jitendra said, "Surely something concrete, because the last IDK was the place where we are standing. The Indian Dancing Klub, which is the only place nearby with a club starting with K. How could we miss it."

Sagar said, "Not alone your fault, we all deserve the credit to this failure."

Ritika said, "Could BUT be another place where he is going to strike again."

Jitendra said, "If he is following a pattern, then BUT is surely the place of next murder."

Sagar winced, "I don't know if he is following a pattern or not, but his MO is same. All I am sure is, that he will strike again. Ladies and Gentlemen we have a Serial Killer on loose."

After a long Delhi Police now have to deal with a Serial Killer. IDK wasn't I Don't Know, but it was Indian Dancing Klub, a popular place in Delhi to hang out. Despite of being a popular joint it didn't crossed the minds of anyone in the department. Well they weren't to blame, as Arvind's murder had no connection whatsoever with this club. The only pattern was that on the night of murder he had gone to some club, Cozy Kitchen. This was the only link which could have been established.

Sagar was furious on himself on how couldn't he have given it a thought that this might be a work of a serial killer. The kind of death Arvind had, and leaving the trace behind in form of a message could only be done by a psycho serial killer. On one side youngsters of Delhi were already hooked on to this murder investigation just by the mere thought of a Serial Killer being involved, while on the other side grown ups of the city were little scared thinking a killer was on loose. Team Sagar returned back to the Akbar Nagar Police Station where already there were hordes of Media people trying to take a byte from the Lead Detective. Sagar ignored them all to rush inside his cabin. They sat.

Jitendra said, "Both of our victims are club goers. Is that the reason why this IDK killer is targeting them. I mean he could be an extremist religionist, who is trying to force morality in Delhi."

Ritika laughed and then concealed her smile, "Come on Arvind hardly used to go to clubs. Didn't his wife Ashima said so. It was just once in blue moon."

Jitendra said, "Yes, once in blue moon is also enough for Psychos."

Sagar said, "Arvind and Faisal had something in common, but not the club angle. So better we gear up ourselves to do some digging."

Jitendra said, "What if they don't have, and this psycho is killing people randomly."

Sagar said, "In that case we should be double geared up."

Jitendra and Ritika nodded, while they got on to digging about the history of Faisal. There was something peculiar about these murders, that the killer was following a chain. If this was a random killing, then the killer shouldn't have left that IDK mark on the wall. He knew what he was doing, and he was boldly challenging the Delhi Police. With a pattern like this, the chances were very high that Faisal and Arvind had some connection in between, a connection that has driven this IDK killer mad enough to kill them. Somewhere down the line there was some secret, or say a profound motive that was driving this killer.

Sagar turned on the television, to only see Media mocking the police work. They were actually calling police, bunch of idiots. An idiot would only not decipher IDK to be the Indian Dancing Klub, when all these places were in close vicinity. Sagar thought that with the resources in hand, media should be thankful that this IDK killer was not carrying an assault gun massacring everyone on street. A Senior Police Officer had escorted Faisal's brother, Imran to meet Sagar. Imran wanted to meet the investigating officer on this case. He clearly looked shattered.

Sagar said, "I am truly sorry for your loss, of which a part is our failure."

Imran said, "No detective, even I had been following the first IDK murder, and despite of knowing that my brother was a regular at Indian Dancing Klub, I couldn't match the two. But what devastates me the most is, that I couldn't help my brother when he needed me."

Sagar said, "Stay strong Imran, we will catch this pig."

Imran said, "I can't even imagine what pain my brother must have got when this IDK killer would have stabbed my Brother, again and again. This killer is a monster, Detective."

Imran then held Sagar's hand, in his and said, "Promise me, you will catch him. You will do better than your best."

Sagar sighed, "You have my word, this killer would die in prison or on gallows."

Imran left, while Sagar stood there with two promises that he had made, first to Ashima and now to Imran. During his job as a detective, Sagar had made many promises to many people, and the good part was that most of the times he had lived up to his promises. But this time was different. These clues, IDK, BUT, this killer was actually talking to the investigating officer, which was Sagar. Sagar didn't want to, not at this point, but was taking this investigation personally. Killer wanted to out smart Sagar, which was unacceptable. This killer was making fun of the entire Law and order of the city. This was unacceptable.

A wise man had said, life will throw you many challenges, but sometimes you got to catch them and throw them back to life. This was exactly what Sagar was thinking. He had to do his best, not just because of Imran or because of Ashima, but for what he was, a police officer. The autopsy results have came in, while Jitendra got the reports to Sagar's cabin.

Jitendra said, "Work of same killer, Check. Blood with which the BUT has been painted, is of Faisal, check. The knife used to kill Arvind and Faisal are same, Check."

Jitendra continued, "But this time the IDK killer stabbed Imran 10 times. One Plus than before."

Ritika said, "By this can we infer, that next victim will have 11 blows."

Sagar said, "The knife is same, so probably we wont get the murder weapon, as he is using it for every other murder. Could knife be something special to him, or what."

Jitendra smiled, "Only if he is a chef. As autopsy team had clarified, this is a kitchen knife."

Sagar said, "Call the autopsy guy, I have some questions."

Sagar hoped that this IDK Killer who was using kitchen knife better not be a bored housewife. The foresight of Sagar was now scanning something being left behind in the bodies of these victims. You know a wise cop, yes cop, not a wise man had said, that dead bodies might be not useful to victim's family but are a treasure of evidences for a cop. He was damn right. This IDK killer had managed to execute these killings without leaving DNA trace, but then he was not a god, but just a human who are prone to make mistakes.

Sagar had known that this time it would be more difficult for him to crack this BUT, as killer must sure have leveled up the game. These psycho killers do this all the time. For them killing a person is not a crime, but a means to derive pleasure and enjoyment. It was the first time Sagar was dealing with a serial killer, but he had known to his guts that he couldn't afford to fail. This wasn't ego, but the spirit that Sagar had in him. The autopsy guy was in the cabin of Sagar.

The autopsy guy, Nitin was feeling little scared as if he had done something wrong, and was caught by the investigative officer. Sagar smiled to get him a seat. They sat and talked.

Sagar said, "What was the knife made of, Ceramic, Steel, Iron, or maybe another metal."

Nitin smiled, "Just a regular kitchen knife detective, a steel one."

Sagar said, "You also did the first autopsy right. Could you recall by the nature of the wounds inflicted if this knife was new, or had been used in the kitchen before."

Nitin nodded, "Brilliant question detective, I think I should have added this in report. Yes it was a new knife, as I had carefully sampled the DNA around wounds, and there was no plant based traces."

Sagar said, "If asked, can you exactly draw the shape of knife, as you would assume it to be."

Nitin said, "Sure thing detective, I will do that, and get it sent to you."

Sagar smiled while Nitin left. Not having the murder weapon didn't meant that the police was clueless if the murder happened with a blow of breath. With a picture of the knife, at least Sagar would know what they were dealing with. It was now that Team Sagar was feeling that they might have taken the first intimate step towards the killer. In police world there was nothing like a small lead, or a big lead, every lead towards catching of the killer was regarded equally important as it had the same potential to bust the criminals.

Sagar was hoping hard, that his move got them closer to the killer. It was strange on how Sagar was sitting in Akbar Nagar Police Station trying to catch the IDK Killer, while IDK killer must be sitting somewhere secret hatching his plan of killing his next victim. Both were racing against each other, and certainly there would be only one winner in this race. This game was no secret, media knew it, people knew it, everyone knew it. So stakes were really high for Sagar, this time. He knew it, Jitendra knew it, and Ritika knew it too. They sat and talked.

Sagar said, "IDK BUT, or can I rephrase it as I don't know, but."

Ritika said, "Apart from giving us clues, he is also trying to send across a message."

Jitendra said, "In that case I am not interested in what his message his, because by the completion of his message, we will have god knows how many dead bodies."

Sagar said, "But what could be his message. IF we crack it before, maybe we might be able to save other people from dying. I know it is all very vague, like I don't know but. I am just out of words."

Ritika said, "So we are detective, it could be anything, even English Professors would not be able to crack this."

Sagar said, "Anyways, just assign this complete the blanks to some junior officer, who is damn good at English, lets see what he sees out of this. Keep me looped in."

I don't know, but, I mean it might have been the clue but the possibilities were infinite. It could be anything in plain English. The truth was that no matter how good a police officer might have been in English, this was hard to decipher. But then it didn't mean that Sagar would surrender.

The deliberate construction of these messages being so cryptic was an indicator that the IDK killer had done lots of homework before preparing this message. Look at the IDK, it was sure that IDK meant I don't Know, and it also meant, Indian Dancing Klub. This was no coincidence but deliberate usage of words in the message. This IDK killer was damn smart, and though unofficially but now Sagar had admitted that he had balls too, because this second murder was committed in broad daylight. How many killers in Delhi would have such courage to kill someone in daylight in city of 1 crore plus people. This man knew his game. Team Sagar were on their way to meet Imran. He was the only person who could have thrown some light into the life of Faisal. They sat together in Faisal's home.

Sagar said, "Imran its very important for us to know, if Faisal had any enmity."

Imran smiled, "Detective we have some properties in the area that are rented out, and never in decades we had a late payment. Faisal used to handle it, so there were no grievances against him. In our locality everyone liked him, not one angry neighbor."

Sagar exhaled, "He was a regular in Indian Dancing Klub right. Did he used to go alone."

Imran said, "Faisal had not visited that place in last 6 or 7 months, but this time he was very excited, as he was going to meet somebody."

Sagar said, "Like a girlfriend or what."

Imran sighed, "Girls were his only weakness. Yes I believe that must have been a girl. Wait, I might have something that might be of help. Will be back in a minute"

The missing links of this investigation were now coming on surface. There do was someone involved in bringing Faisal to that Indian Dancing Klub. A wise man had said, every family has a secret about their family member. This family was no different. Faisal was still a bachelor until he died, while Imran his younger brother had a beautiful wife and two small kids who were constantly peeking from behind the curtain into the living room. The innocence on their face had made the day of Detective Sagar.

Imran returned back with a laptop, it was personal laptop of Faisal. Imran being a brother had known the password and sites he visited. He opened, the website named Ginger. Imran stumbled upon a message and showed it to Detective Sagar.

Sagar said, "So it was a girl named Reshma, who had called Faisal that day, interesting."

Chapter 6

A wise man had said that every crime has a story behind it, and probably Reshma was the story behind Faisal's death. It was because of this girl that Faisal had gone to that Indian Dancing Klub. It was strange, as the profile of Reshma said that she was only 22, while Faisal was much older than her. Why would young Reshma show that much interest in old Faisal. All doubts apart, why would Reshma call Faisal to just this place IDK? Something was murky. Sagar had already detected a foul play. This was just but a trap, and possibly Reshma was an accomplice to this IDK killer. Or who knew that this profile of Reshma was fake just to trap Faisal in his own death trap.

Sagar was thankful that he came to meet Imran and this revelation came out which probably could have been gone under the shades. Sagar had taken the laptop of Faisal and given it to the IT department to track back this Reshma. Sagar was hopeful that he would hit on something with this lead. Maybe this was the first mistake that this IDK killer had made. Maybe this was the beginning of the end of this IDK killer. As every cop would say no crime is perfect, neither was this one. Meanwhile Team Sagar sat in the police station.

Jitendra said, "So this IDK killer might not be working alone."

Ritika said, "That is too early to say, this Reshma could just be another bot that this IDK killer created."

Sagar said, "There is another angle apart from the identity of Reshma. Why did this IDK killer called Faisal to Indian Dancing Klub. Why only this club, and leave the initials as a clue. This club has far greater connection to our killings than we are thinking."

Jitendra said, "Maybe something happened in this club in past."

Sagar said, "Now you are getting at it. I think we need to check the past of this club, and see if it has any connection to Faisal and Arvind."

A wise cop had said, that crimes are like festivals in some way, because they all happen for a reason. It was no secret that every murder had a motive. In this case the writing of IDK on that wall also had a motive behind. This Indian Dancing Klub was concealing a big secret underneath. Maybe in past Arvind and Faisal have visited this club and were part of some dirty doing.

Arvind and Faisal didn't knew each other, or their families would have mentioned. So what was the thing that connected them. The biggest why was on why did this IDK killer gave importance to this IDK. You know IDK had a history, of being a perfect hang out place for couples. Then why Arvind and Faisal, as clearly they weren't gay to have visited the place as a couple, so was there any other girl involved. This could have been a possibility. Maybe a love triangle from past, but then how could Faisal and Arvind not know each other. This was all very overwhelming for Sagar.

They have reached the IDK, the spot of the second murder. They soon got attended by the Manager who recognized Team Sagar from the other day.

Manager said, "Officers, how can we be of help. Trust me even we want to get rid of this IDK killer. You know this murder has harmed our business a lot."

Sagar said, "Sorry to hear that. But here is a picture of Arvind. The first victim of IDK killer, do you by any chance recognize him."

Manager shook his head, "Detective, I have seen him in news. He has never been to this place."

Sagar said, "Okay then tell me about Faisal, from when he is visiting this place, and what he does when here."

Manager smiled, "Ah, Mr. Faisal was a real regular and a true loyal. He has been visiting this place since he was teen. But as long as I have seen him, he used to sit in that corner seat, have drinks, and enjoy seeing couples dance together on the stage. At many instances he had offered free drinks to many couples."

Sagar said, "So he was a regular since his teens. Is there anybody in your staff to have witnessed all those years of Faisal coming down to your club."

Manager gave a huge winning smile while he took Team Sagar towards the back of the club. Sagar too was having this smile but inside. He has seen many such cases of murder where the lead felt to be good and intuitive, but turns up cold when it comes to actually remembering the facts. The image of Faisal of being an innocent victim was distorted in the head of Detective Sagar. He was one of those flamboyant men who always sought love but never the responsibilities attached to it. Imran might not have clearly said it, but he did that Faisal was weak to women. It was enough to tell what Faisal did coming to this club, in hopes of actually finding someone whom he could have a fling or maybe affair with. By offering those free drinks to couples he only sought attention of the female side of couples. It wouldn't come of as a surprise to Sagar if it got revealed that Faisal had a dark secret from past in regards to an affair with some woman.

They had entered the back office of IDK. It was a small room but had many old faces sitting there. One of them was Kishore, he was once a manager of this club, but by his old age was transferred to the accounts section. Sagar could tell by his age that he had seen it all.

Sagar said, "Nice to meet you sir, we hope you are keeping pace with IDK killings."

Kishore said, "You are here to know about Faisal right."

Sagar nodded while Kishore continued, "Well he was a regular to our club. I could never forget his flirty nature. He used to hit on women when young, offer them drinks and ask randomly to dance on stage. In fact sometimes I even warned him of not doing so with consequences of being banned from the club. You know how conservative we were during those times. Not just this club but the entire country."

Sagar nodded, "Can some of those girl be the reason of his murder now."

Kishore said, "Those were like, as you cops say, open and shut cases. No one would have hold that grudge for so long. Least what I can recall from my memory."

Sagar said, "Here is my card, in case if you remember anything. Thanks for the help though."

This was quite a revelation, apart from being flamboyant, Faisal was also nudgy towards women. There was deep gut feeling of Sagar that these IDK killing might have something to do with younger days of Faisal. But unfortunately he didn't had any proof to back up his theory. The conversation Sagar had with this old man Kishore, had no red flags. Flirting in clubs is like abuses in police station, very common. What didn't made sense and pinched Sagar was that one night nudge would not be enough for such a prolonged sense of justice. It was related to some girl with whom Faisal had a deeper and intimate relationship. Such hate couldn't come out of flings, there had to be some greater explanation to this.

It struck Sagar, that if Imran knew Faisal's passwords, then he would also sure know about the relationships that

Faisal had in past. It was time to meet the brother in angst. Team Sagar was headed to meet Imran. A wise man had said, if you love something then never let it go, because when feelings strike they strike harder. Team Sagar was sitting with Imran in his house.

Sagar said, "You said that Faisal had weakness for women, what did you meant."

Imran smiled, "If Faisal sees a beautiful woman he would fall for her easily, that is what I meant."

Sagar nodded, "Imran I need you to think hard and recall every relationship that your brother had. Not the crushes, but in instances where your brother hung out with those women, or had an intimate relationship with. It is very important for this investigation."

Imran sighed, "I have names of all of them on my tongue tip. Least of all the girlfriends my brother ever mentioned. One is Aditi, and the other is Nazreen. They are the only two with whom the relationship ever lasted."

Sagar patted Imran, "Great, now help me with their addresses."

There it was Aditi and Nazreen, one Hindu and other a Muslim girl. After all, Faisal had turned out to be quite a secular guy. But how could a man having weakness for girls had only two girlfriends in all of his life. Though Faisal died way before his natural death, but still this number was a little miss fit. A wise man had said that if you get everything you want, the purpose of life would cease to exist. Sagar was happy that least he had got two leads. It is said that there are some secrets which a man shares only with his partner. Faisal was not married to them but still they qualified to know much more about Faisal than what Team Sagar was being fed with.

Team Sagar was headed to meet Aditi who was now married and had 1 kid. Aditi was Faisal's girlfriend during his teen days. Imran had also told them that this affair didn't end well. So it was not wrong to suspect if Aditi or her present family had something to do with Faisal's death. The only thing which didn't fit well was why would Arvind be killed for this affair. All these questions had clouded Sagar's head, and the answers were only with one woman for now, Aditi herself. They sat opposite each other, while Aditi's husband resorted to another room.

Sagar said, "Aditi I have no intentions of disturbing your married life, but I have some questions."

Aditi sighed, "You must know that I haven't had contact with Faisal in over a decade."

Sagar said, "When you both broke up, did Faisal ever bothered you, or maybe asserted his love over you in a wrong way. I hope you are getting what I am trying to ask."

Aditi smiled, "He might not look like a gentleman, but in his heart he was. I think you don't know our story properly. There was no rift in between us. We wanted to get married. But then you must know how a marriage prospects of a Hindu girl and a Muslim Boy are. Our families totally shut our possibilities to get married. My brother even got in a fight with Faisal to which Faisal never reacted. When I was about to get married finally, Faisal even wished me best. He was not that kind of man Detective."

Sagar said, "You said that your brother beat him up, was that the end of it."

Aditi said, "Yes that ended right there. Now my brother is in US, for last 8 years. Do you think he could have a part in killing of Faisal. Wait, i still have some things that connect me back to Faisal, maybe they could help."

Aditi went inside, while Sagar waited and sipped on to the tea he was presented. Aditi's husband tried taking the glimpse of the room by passing through. He was clearly curious, and why would not he be. Aditi had apparently shared everything with her husband including her affair with Faisal. So least he was not shocked, but still worried if Police might drag Aditi in this investigation which would only defame their family name.. Sagar even smiled at her husband, to which he too smiled back.

A wise man had said, a woman never reveals all her secrets until she is done with the man. The conversation they had suggested that Aditi was clearly over with Faisal. Sagar could understand on how he had just brought back the old memories to Aditi. It was always not nice to meet with Police discussing about your first love's murder while your husband is in a room beside. These were situations that probably gave birth to words like awkward. Aditi was back, and she was holding a photo album. These must been pictures of Aditi with Faisal. Now this might be of help.

Aditi said, "All our memories are in this album."

Sagar saw and recognized one from IDK and said, "What was so special about you both visiting IDK."

Aditi felt back, "Special, that was the best place for couples to hang out back then. Of course it was special. Ask any body from our generation, or ask yourself, if you are from Delhi."

Sagar nodded, "This is important, please try remember if anything went wrong in IDK on one of Faisal's visit there. Or if Faisal mentioned to you about any such thing back then."

Aditi said, "Nothing I could remember of, but yes. Sagar and I met in IDK our first time, and it was habit of Sagar to hit on girls, in that club. I hope this helps."

Sagar exhaled, "Yes it does, Aditi. Here is my card, if you remember anything else."

Well not all of it was a surprise. Sagar had known Faisal to be a flamboyant lover boy after the feed from IDK managers. Someone who visited IDK even to this age could not have a different personality than this. But now it was official that Faisal used to hit on girls in that club. So maybe before his affair with Aditi, or after her affair with Aditi, he might have picked the wrong girl for whom he was avenged now. But again, where did Arvind came in between all of this.

The link between Arvind and Faisal which was missing was the biggest headache that Sagar had encountered till now in this investigation. They were headed to Nazreen's house. The second lead who could have shed some light on this IDK angle of the case. All Sagar was worried about was what if another murder happened before he could get a hold of this investigation. With every second passing, there was a looming disaster which Sagar wanted to avert. They were sitting opposite to each other. Nazreen too had a family and her husband had for now gone to work.

Nazreen said, "I was done with Faisal, so why bother me now."

Sagar said, "We are just here for few questions, that is all. How and why did you and Faisal Broke up."

Nazreen sighed, "As you are investigating his death, I assume you must have known what kind of person he was. Not in a bad sense, but he was way ahead of his times. Faisal never really got to forget his first love, Aditi. Sometimes even with me, he used to talk about her. Anyways, we were in love. Then I asked him to marry me, but he refused, and said that let us live the rest of our lives as lovers, and if I wanted we could also move in together. See detective, I belong to a very conservative family, hence I had to move on."

Sagar sighed, "Fair enough. Do you remember anything like a beef Faisal had with someone, or some strange incidence that might have happened with him in IDK."

Nazreen said, "Detective he was a regular of IDK, but never did anything like a beef happened."

Nazreen said, "Don't leave already, let me get you some tea."

Team Sagar then sat back, while Nazreen went inside to make some tea. The hopes that Sagar had on Nazreen on finding the IDK angle was turning up dead. Maybe the very theory of Sagar was bogus that IDK had a deeper connection to these killings. But it was also absurd on why did Faisal always visited that place. In his teenage days Sagar might have understood the intentions. But even up till now, when kids half his age visited that place, it was little hard to digest. Something somewhere was very wrong, and Sagar had to find it, before this IDK killer struck again. Nazreen was back with tea in her hands and smile on her face. There do was some pain in her eyes, maybe the sorrow of losing her ex love.

A wise man had said, that easiest to remember and hardest to forget thing in this world is love. He was so damn right. They were having sip of tea, when Nazreen put her cup down to gaze back at Sagar.

Nazreen said, "Wait, there might be something of help. After we broke up, it took me two years to get married, in those two years I met Faisal couple of times. Oddly in that place IDK. I even asked him, are you looking for some other girl in this place, to which he said no. It was weird then I asked, why was he still visiting IDK. It was then Faisal said, I am waiting for someone and some things to make up for."

Team Sagar glanced a look while Sagar said, "Great, did he tell any name."

Nazreen said, "It was long back and we had broken up, so I didn't care asking him that."

Sagar finished his cup and said, "You have helped us more than you think."

Jitendra and Ritika also nodded with Sagar while they left. He do was waiting for someone, someone to whom he had done bad, or why would he want to make things right with someone. This someone had to be the IDK killer. The broken links were again getting connected, meanwhile Jitendra got a call.

Jitendra said, "Detective its double good news. We have a location for Reshma."

Chapter 7

A wise man had said that a criminal is only as smart as the cop allows him to be. That was so apt. After all the meticulous work by the IT team of Akbar Nagar Police station, now Team Sagar had a location of this girl Reshma who was apparently the reason why Faisal went to Indian Dancing Klub. Whether Reshma was a conspirer of this murder or not, she sure now was a person of interest. Sagar was sure that Reshma would get them closer to the IDK killer some way or the other.

The clock was ticking, as Sagar knew that BUT murder was not the last deed of this IDK killer, as the message was still incomplete. Team Sagar was headed to the location of Reshma. The chances were slim, but Reshma could also have been the girl whom Faisal wanted to make up to, or maybe she shared the same name in pretence. The only miss fit was the fact that Reshma was too young to have a tryst with Faisal during his teen days. Anyways, all these questions were to be answered soon. Vehicle of Sagar stopped while they stepped out to the address of Reshma. Then all their hopes turned cringe worthy. After all this time, they hit with this.

Sagar said, "So the location of Reshma is a cyber café."

Jitendra disappointingly said, "Detective I have no idea that the location was of a cyber café. Of course this IDK killer would not be that stupid."

Sagar sighed, "I wonder if Reshma is even a real person, rather a fake id made from some café."

Sagar's hope were all down, but since they were here, Sagar wanted to take a dig in this café, in hopes that maybe this IDK killer was unguarded while coming here and left some clue. They entered the café. It was a huge one and was crowded with tech savvy kids. It must have been rush hour, as Sagar didn't even see a single vacant system. If this rush was pertinent at most of its working hours then expecting the owner to remember the face of IDK killer was some fantasy for Delhi Police.

Sagar reached out for the owner of the cyber café, while Jitendra and Ritika teetered the place in hopes they find somebody suspicious. Of course they weren't hoping that they will stumble upon the IDK killer, but the chances of finding a regular patron doing illegal work was the best shot to juggle the place down. The owner was an old man, Jagat. Apparently the cyber café was also named on him, Jagat Cyber Café, not very novel but conventional.

Sagar said, "Hello Mr. Jagat I am Detective Sagar, and here to ask you few questions, as probably the IDK killer who is doing rounds in news, might have come here and used your computer to create a fake profile on Ginger."

Jagat said, "Oh anything that I could be helpful with, apart from remembering a face."

Sagar looked around and said, "Do you have CCTV's in here."

Jagat winked, "I am sorry detective, but this place is kind of old fashioned."

Sagar said, "Do you remember, anyone looking suspicious coming down to your café on 5th of this month. Anyone with a hoodie, or a cap on his head with glasses.. All I mean is, someone trying to hide his face. ".

Jagat said, "I am sorry detective, but your description doesn't matches to our visitors. But if you want, you can make one of your IT member sit on the system he used."

Sagar smiled at the old man for making sense and being cooperative. Sagar summoned his IT team to the cyber café, while Jagat rounded up the crowd to leave with a mention of ongoing police work. That was a helpful gesture by this old man, sabotaging his business for law and order. He sure did lived on the reputation of this place being little old fashioned. Deep down Sagar was hoping that this Reshma be a real person, because catching real people was way far more easy than hitting heads on computers with a faceless criminal behind. The only hope that IT team had for now was that while creating the fake id of Reshma, this IDK killer might have accessed his mail maybe, or some other personal account on some website. This was the best shot that the IT team had.

The IT team soon figured which computer was used, and they have got to their examination. Hours went by, but they were unable to find anything from that session, during that time of chat. Finally IT team took the system with them for a detailed surgery. Meanwhile Team Sagar had a little chat amongst, while they stood near the entrance of café.

Sagar said, "If not until now, I fear we will find anything in the computer."

Ritika said, "I agree, if a man can plan murders like that he would sure not be stupid to leave traces like his personal email id or opening some of his other personal accounts."

Jitendra said, "But wait, didn't Imran said that he heard Faisal talking with Reshma the other day."

It struck Sagar, "You are right, which means, there do is some girl involved. Tell the IT team."

Jitendra said, "Maybe we weren't all that wrong all this time."

The short lost hope was back in Team Sagar's camp, while IT team was briefed that instead of a man, a woman might have used the computer so they look accordingly. It was already late, while Sagar took off to his home. For past couple of days he was unable to catch up with his family, and was sure that Sarika would welcome him with a grumpy face. But that was just a shade of the day. The pleasure of catching up with the joy of his son Arjun was far greater than any tantrum Sarika would throw at him.

This IDK killer was killing the peace of Sagar's life. During past week all Sagar had pondered about was these IDK killings, and nothing else. The more Sagar thought about this IDK killer the more Sagar's conviction was intensifying to catch him. This was the beauty of a relationship between a detective and a criminal. Sagar was back at home, and yes he was right to have been welcomed by Sarika with a grumpy face. She said nothing and just went inside after opening the door, while face of Arjun got lit up, who was doing his homework in the living room.

Sagar said, "Hey how us my champ doing."

Arjun smiled broadly, "Great dad, but where were you in these last days, and did you got to catch the IDK killer. Tell you what that all my friends ask me about it since I have told you are investigating this case."

Sagar exhaled, "Come on you shouldn't be talking about crimes in school. It's not cool."

Arjun said, "Even talking about the catching of a criminal, is not cool."

Sagar sighed while Arjun got back doing his homework. Sagar made a cup of coffee for himself, as he didn't wanted to bother Sarika and start another argument. There were times when these couple were newly married and couldn't even wait to talk to each other on strike of every hour. That was then, and this was now. Sometimes Sagar thought that he was with a completely different woman, than whom he had married. The feeling was mutual with Sarika, who thought that she was with a different man with whom she had married.

They talked less, and there were piles of misunderstanding between the two. The only good part about their marriage was that it was still on, and they were still loyal to each other. Call it blessing or the connection between the two. Night dawned and Sagar was resting in the bedroom reading a true crime book written by one of his senior officer, when Sarika came in.

Sarika said, "Assuming that you took out some time to visit our home, you must have also got the time to think about sending Arjun to boarding school."

Sagar exhaled, "Not now Sarika, please."

Sarika said, "What exactly, not now. Sending Arjun to boarding school or talking about it with me"

Sagar said, "Actually both. Don't you see how happy Arjun is in home, and also doing well in studies. Don't ruin it. We will manage somehow. And trust me, boarding schools are not meant for everyone. I don't think Arjun is going to like it. Plus he is too young to be left alone on his own. He got to first develop the understanding of what is right for him and what is wrong."

Sarika said, "Just for the record, I am taking that promotion in my office, which will mean more working hours. So you better come up with something to balance the time with Arjun. Good Night."

Sagar nodded, "Yeah, it was nice talking to you too."

A wise man had said that responsibilities are like ascending age of a person, which you never ask for but still you get them. Already IDK killer had troubled Sagar enough, given him morning headaches and now Sarika was giving him chills. Life for Sagar wasn't easy. A new day had dawned with the same lurking danger of another IDK killing. There were already rounds of news calling the Delhi Police incompetent right on National television even in morning shows. On the other hand Sagar was still unable to forget the graffiti in blood, first IDK and then BUT.

This IDK killer must have thoroughly planned his killings well before hand. But how can plans be so deliberate and aligned so well with reality. For now what was important was what BUT stood for. It was the key to stop another murder. Just like IDK, this BUT concealed the location of third murder. Yes the threat of third murder was true, and Team Sagar couldn't have ignored it. But what actually was the other meaning of BUT, it wasn't an acronym like IDK. So was it just BUT. This was where the Delhi Police was getting beaten up by the odds. Team Sagar kept on the discussion about this BUT.

Sagar said, "So what have our English grand masters come to a conclusion with."

Jitendra said, "Many, possibilities Detective. But not one of a certain, though we aren't able to crack the complete sentence yet. But we have got some matches for BUT."

Ritika said, "It could be, Before ur Turn, Behind ur Turf, Beneath your Tree, and Back in Ugly Time."

Sagar said, "Wait, Beneath your tree, aint all victims were found dead under a tree."

Jitendra said, "That is true, so is this the clue which Killer is giving us."

Sagar though for a while, "Another thing which we know is that this score belongs to ugly past. But clearly the killer is trying to give us the location, so I think it is probably Behind ur Turf."

Team Sagar glanced each other, while they knew that they might have hit the right spot, or maybe somewhere near.

I mean this was it, Behind ur turf, this could be the most appropriate challenge for the police. Some place where the police had its utmost authority. This time IDK killer was going to make his murder spot too intimate. Wasn't this the style of all serial killers. First they show what they are made of, and then they mock what the police is made of. This killer was now going to mock the entire police force of Delhi.

Twice was enough for any normal murderer to have ended up in prison, but the third time meant that the killer was smarter than the police. Sagar was right that this time it was going to be somewhere near the police existence. Of all things that Sagar had known about this killer was that he was fearless, and would never miss a chance to attract the attention of the police, people and media. By doing this third murder in police turf would certainly attract lots of eyeballs, exactly what this killer was in pursuit of.

Jitendra said, "Detective, in that case what could be the location."

Sagar said, "I don't know if I am right, but behind our police station there is a small park, and I am getting a strong feeling that third murder will happen there."

Ritika said, "After your strong argument I am getting the same bad feeling."

Sagar said, "We need to buckle up guys, sanction a police unit to canvass the park 24*7."

Jitendra said, "But what if we are wrong."

Sagar sighed, "This is a chance we have to take. I know we are outnumbered on the resources, but this is the best we have got. Also tell the police units to be cautious near the borders of Akbar Nagar Police jurisdiction."

The threat was inevitable and all the nightmares of Delhi Police would come true if this third murder happened. Just one man, or maybe woman, who might be the IDK killer, had stirred the sleep of South Delhi Police. Just one killer committing murder in living areas, parks and near busy places like clubs had put questions on their ability. If someone was to ask Sagar personally then it was a shame on the mettle of Delhi Police. In a city which was covered with most numbers of CCTV cameras, this was shameful that police was unable to track down a murderer.

There were rounds that soon CBI was to take over this investigation. In his heart Sagar knew that this was not a rumor, and at the same time he wished that before CBI stepped in they be able to wrap up the case. If CBI stepped in, people will lose faith. Sagar never in his career had so badly wanted a criminal. Sagar wanted this killer as badly as his wife wanted Arjun to be sent to boarding school. He was curious to know the identity of this killer who had given sleepless nights to Delhi Police. Team Sagar sat in his cabin while the IT guy came in.

IT guy said, "Detective, I think I have a good news for you."

Jitendra said, "Well that is rare these days, so why don't you start by spilling it."

IT guy said, "We did a thorough search of the system with time stamps of the messages that were sent to Faisal. In one of the time stamps, we found that log in was made into the official cyber café software of the place. It means that Reshma is one if the employees of that Café."

Sagar said, "Okay, any idea who exactly she could be."

IT guy said, "That is another good news. See this Ginger Dating app has a messenger service too, and in one of the instances, this Reshma had sent a voice message to Faisal. We have that recording. Now if we match the voices of all the female staff of the café to this recording, maybe we can catch that woman."

Sagar glanced at Jitendra and Ritika, said, "What are we then waiting for."

Now Reshma would no longer be a mystery girl. It was just a matter of matching the voices. Jagat Cyber Café also had some staff who apparently looked after the Xerox section of the café, did graphic designing, and did typing work. Sagar was in the café and had taken Jagat to a corner to know about the staff. There were 5 female staff in the café, and certainly one of them was the aide to the killer. The plan was simple, Police would not tell the female staff that they were looking for a voice sample, but rather that they wanted to record the statement of all staff members. This way the workers wouldn't get alarmed and would enable the recording of their unadulterated voice.

By mere dropping of the police in the café had sure alarmed the staff members, but it was hard to tell by the reactions who it was, as everyone was rebuked. Soon an interrogation room was set, and one by one the staff members were called. Just to make it look genuine, first the male staff was called and they did gave their statements which were recorded by the police just for formality, then came the turn of female staff. They came in.

Ruchika said, "As I have already told the police, that day I was working on a client designing order. I was submerged in work and didn't see anything."

Neeta said, "A guy with a hoodie can be anyone. I mean many customers here come in hoodies."

Preet said, "I wasn't working that day."

Namita said, "I am not sure if I have seen anyone matching that description."

Jiya said, "I don't know why police is hassling me. I mean you people need to check the CCTV footage of nearby shops as we don't have one, maybe you all will get the killer. But seriously do not expect us to be the CCTV eyes of police department. It is very hard to remember every customer that walks in. Period"

The last one was the most touching testimony given by any of the staff members. The recordings were now transferred to the laptop of the IT guy. Sagar was hoping hard that they find the aide to the killer least this time. Catching Reshma was the next best thing to catch the IDK killer. All eyes were set on the Software that was analyzing the voice sample, and bingo there came a match.

IT Guy smiled, "That wimpy girl Preet is your Reshma."

Chapter 8

A wise man had said, if you commit a crime, you put your sub conscious hanging in middle situation for ever. How true it was. Right from the start Preet was acting a little weird. At first, it didn't raise any brows of the Delhi Police considering that any normal person who was to undergo a police statement would act a little weird. But she committed two mistakes, one of not being able to understand that her voice sample was being taken, which was understandable, considering that an aide to IDK killer would only be stupid, as what person with normal IQ would help a serial killer. Her second mistake was that she actually lied in front of police that she was not working that day, as Sagar had attendance records of all the employees.

Her voice was a 98% match, which was way above the benchmark to be considered as an evidence. Jagat dispersed all the employees but asked Preet to stay in the interrogation room. Her intuition had already whispered in her ears, that she was caught. No innocent person would sweat in an air conditioned room, but Preet was. What she didn't comprehend was that how was she caught. Team Sagar came in with relentless attitude.

Sagar said, "What should we call you, Preet or Reshma or a sidekick to IDK killer."

Preet made frowning face, "What are you talking about detective, I know nothing about this IDK killer."

Sagar said, "Oh understood, but you sure knew Faisal."

Jitendra said, "Or maybe detective, she doesn't knows IDK killer because she herself is the one, right."

Preet trembled, "Look I have nothing to do with these killings, trust me."

Sagar said, "I will rather trust on the voice sample of yours which we found in the messenger section of Faisal from a girl named Reshma. Trust me Reshma, oh Preet, this evidence is enough to put you up in prison for a very long time. If I were you, I would have started talking."

She felt her stomach churning, and was terrified of even hearing those words of being sent to prison. Trust me Indian prisons are the worst places where a person could find themselves in, especially for women. Sagar had seen those expressions all his life. Now she recalled sending that voice message to Faisal. Damn she must have felt naïve. She might have deleted that voice recording from the computer she used as Reshma but she clearly missed out deleting the recording from the chat box.

Team Sagar left the room to only stand at the door as Sagar wanted to give her some time to think what hell of a situation she had dragged herself in. Team Sagar talked loudly about what all charges they were going to put on Preet or rather Reshma. There were legal clauses and jargons that Preet had never heard about but they sounded terrifying. Jitendra was the one who was asserting that they blamed both the killings on Preet. Deep down they knew that such a lean girl like Preet was incapable of murdering two men, but they also had a job to do to find what actually went behind the scenes. They wanted to know what angle Preet had in these killings. Right now Preet was the best catch that the detectives had. Preet called them from inside, in a soft, nimble and innocent voice.

Preet said, "I will tell you everything, but in return I don't want any charges to be pressed against me."

Sagar smiled, "This is not a game, you are playing Reshma. We will sure charge you with all wrong you have done. But by starting to speak, you can avoid the charges that are meant for that IDK killer. Getting it"

Preet sighed, "It was just another day, when a man with a long over coat approached me for a writing assignment. He had few hand written documents that he wanted to digitalize. He sat with me all the time I did typing. We talked and soon got on a friendly tone. He then proposed me that I could earn some extra bucks, if I helped him in pranking one of his friends Faisal. Rest I impersonated as Reshma and did everything he told me. I chatted with Faisal and the last step was to call him to IDK. That is just it. When I heard the news of Faisal being killed, I panicked, and tried erasing any tracks that could lead back to me."

Sagar glanced at his team members, "Did you saw his face, and do you remember it."

Preet said, "Though we met only once, but I clearly remember his face. I mean any one could tell that he had a fake beard and fake moustaches. I should have known, he was tricking me in something illicit."

Sagar said to Jitendra, "Call the sketch artist, I want this face on papers."

Good news is always around, sometimes it just takes a while, and now it was in the camp of Team Sagar. Preet had clearly said that the IDK killer was using some make up to hide his real face, but still they would get some rough idea about the make and the face of the killer. Preet was now being taken to the Akbar Nagar Police Station to be processed. While en route, Sagar had assured Preet that he would put some good words for the Judge to be lenient.

After all this toil for days, now Team Sagar would finally have a sketch of the killer's face. A wise man had said, Belief was a matter of perspective and not a thing between two people. Sagar was also furious on how easily this IDK killer had fooled this young girl for an incentive of few handful bucks. This man was dangerous, manipulative and not just smart. Team Sagar was sitting in their den while a police officer came in striding through the door. Without making it obvious Sagar crossed his fingers that it be a good news and not some another murder by this IDK killer. But did he really had that control over fate.

Police Officer said, "Detective there is a man named Salman Butt, who wants to meet you."

Jitendra said, "What is it about."

Police officer said in a strong voice, "He is a friend of Shah Faisal, and his last name is Butt, rest you people are smarter than I am to figure it out."

Team Sagar exchanged a glance, while the police officer went back to bring in Salman Butt. He appeared to be of same age as Faisal and had a strong built. He was looking a little scared, and he should be because this was not any normal investigation of lost cell phone. That feeling was not novel for Sagar, as no one enters a police station with joy and cheer in their heart.

A wise cop had said, that a police station is just but a place where all the troubles come to life. They sat, while Sagar offered him a glass of water. Maybe this man was another link to get closer to the IDK killer.

Salman said, "I know it sounds crazy but I think Faisal was killed because of my wife."

Sagar said, "What make you think that? Your last name being Butt, doesn't justifies this act."

Salman gulped the whole glass, "I and Faisal studied together in college. We used to be best friends, like the ones who would never leave each others sight. But then during the last year of college, a fresher girl came in. Her name was Asma. Soon Asma and I became friends as one day I helped her dropping home in mid of heavy rains. Our friendship grew stronger, and I developed feelings for her. Then one day Faisal confronts me and says that I have to pick one person Asma or Faisal. See we were young, and teenagers. You know that phase of life. So I chose love over friendship. It was that day and day till he died, Faisal deleted me out of his life. This BUT is no coincidence. Since I heard about his death, it has been haunting me like anything."

Sagar exhaled, "What happened between you and Asma then."

Salman said, "She is my wife and mother to our two kids. It was Asma that pushed me to come here, and tell this entire thing to you people."

This was interesting. There was another girl in the story of Faisal, the flamboyant and Casanova Faisal. If Asma would just have been a fling the emotions wouldn't have been any stronger. But what this Salman guy was suggesting maybe this BUT was meant for him, or rather his surname BUTT. But then who really killed Faisal, because Salman would be only person to have avenged his wife and visit police to tell a shammed story, as Faisal had bad eyes on her. Plus considering the entire story, it would have been Salman who should have been killed, and killer should have been Faisal. If this connection was true, then this IDK killer was purely indicating to a woman from past.

Even Nazreen had said, that Faisal used to wait for someone in IDK, for something to make up. Was this person Asma whom he had been waiting for. Sagar for the first time in this entire investigation was feeling impressed on how cryptic the clues of this killer were.. In one word, this killer was sending across several messages. Sagar now looked back at Salman who was now feeling better after shedding this weight of confession from his conscious.

Sagar said, "Did Asma used to visit IDK."

Salman shook his head, "No no no, she is a very family kind of girl. This partying and dancing in public places would be the last thing she would do."

Sagar said, "Could there be any chance that Faisal waited for Asma to come to IDK, so he could make up to his mistakes. Any chance"

Salman said, "In that case he should be waiting for me, and not Asma."

Sagar said, "Was there any other girl from Faisal's past whom he had done wrong, and wanted to make up for that. I mean did he ever mentioned to you about any dirty secret. You know, something on those similar lines."

Salman shook his head, "I don't think so, if there would have been an affair from his past I would have known. He shared everything with me, back when we were friends. And there were no secrets between us. In fact now I remember something he used to say that some secrets are there in place to keep you going. It was just a random thing he said couple of times when we friends used to hang out and play card games."

A wise cop had said that in murder investigation, revelations do just same as a blow of breath do to castle of cards. Just when Sagar had known something about the IDK killer, something new pops up and he had to build the entire assumptions all over again. At this diversion of the investigation again same thing was happening.

Now as per Salman this whole murder was based on the relationship triangle between Faisal, Asma and Salman. Then why did this IDK killer made Arvind his target. There has to be an explanation, as another man had died too. He didn't went on a vacation but to heaven. If writing of that BUT on wall was meant for Salman Butt to come in front of police, and IDK clearly meant Indian Dancing Klub where Faisal was killed, in that case these killings could never be random.

Sagar questioned with rigorous pressure on Salman if he knew Arvind or has seen him somewhere with Faisal or even in IDK, but his answer was just nope. If Arvind didn't knew Asma then the motive of his killing was surely distinct. But Salman showing up in Akbar Nagar Police Station was surely somehow connected to the motive of this murder. Salman left to make a call to his wife Asma, as Sagar had asked him to bring her in for questioning. Team Sagar sat in their den still trying to figure out why that BUT was painted on the wall.

Jitendra said, "I don't know if that BUT was meant for Salman Butt. But I am sure it has clue to where the next murder will happen. I mean these serial killers do not change their patterns or MO."

Ritika said, "I don't know from where this thought came, but could Salman Butt be the next target."

Sagar said, "You are not wrong Ritika, it occurred to me too. I think we should provide protection to Salman till this monster is caught."

Sagar exhaled, "Also I am sure that these killing are happening because of a woman whom Arvind and Faisal both knew. Clearly not Asma"

Jitendra said, "I agree, this could only be the message he is trying to convey."

There was another woman in this mystery, that had a greater role behind the inspiration of these killings, but then who was she. Neither Imran knew anything about a woman or a girl from Faisal's past to have caused such damage, nor did Ashima knew. Arvind and Faisal had never even met with each other. That gut feeling of Sagar was yelling at him in his mind that they might have been misguided in this investigation. The link between Arvind and Faisal was becoming very important to be dug out.

Sagar remembered Ishwar Das, who was the journalist whom they have narrowed it down while searching clues in IDK. He too turned up into a dead lead. It meant that with IDK he only was suggesting one thing, and with BUT too he might be suggesting only one thing. But then how could two coincidences happen in a same murder mystery. It was beyond the understanding of Sagar. Though Salman had already spilled out all the secrets between him and Faisal, but it was important to know the Asma side of story. She came in, and with all that simplicity it didn't even occurred to Sagar if she had ever gone to college and was only home schooled. They sat together.

Sagar said, "Its brave of you Asma to come here. Now tell us if Faisal did something to you which you haven't shared with Salman. It is very important for us to know this."

Asma clichéd, "He was a jerk, and sometimes I even think that its good he was murdered."

Sagar glanced at Jitendra, "Okay we are going somewhere. So why did you think this?"

Asma exhaled, "Initially when I had not known Salman nor Faisal, he appeared to be a nice guy, who didn't used to miss any chance of hitting on me, of course in directly and with decency. But things got exactly opposite since the day I started seeing Salman. He would threaten me when he found me alone, to leave Salman. He threatened me that he would tell my brother that I was sleeping with many men in college and what not. I hope you are getting the picture of what a guy Faisal was."

Sagar said, "Did he ever assaulted you, or tried assaulting you."

Asma smiled, "I may be a simple and down to earth person, but then I am also no Mother Teresa. If he had tried assaulting me, he would be rotting in prison till now, and not have got fortunate enough to be murdered."

Sagar tried asking other questions to Asma but it didn't worked out, as these incidences were from way back past, and Asma had already flushed out all of those bad memories. When Sagar was asking these questions he had kept Salman waiting outside. He didn't want a friend to remember his friend as an antagonist of his life. Sagar had known by all these revelations on how the character of Faisal was, and now it was getting despiteful.

It was also strange that his other two girlfriends didn't have any such cheap incidences with him. Maybe he had a change of heart after Asma incidence. As the other two girlfriends of Faisal's life came in after he had parted his ways with Salman. Sagar escorted Salman and Asma out of the police station with a gesture of thanks. This Butt pair had shed lots of light into the other half personality of Faisal. He was not just a lover boy after all, but a psycho lover boy. Maybe this incidence with Asma was something that this IDK killer was referring too. Sagar was also glad that people like Salman existed, who despite of knowing that a person was unpleasant to their wife, should also get justice. Team Sagar was sitting again with a cup of coffee opening their sealed lips.

Jitendra said, "So what do you think Detective, about this possessive side of Faisal."

Sagar said, "I have this very strong gut feeling that this possessive side of Faisal was something that the IDK killer wanted us to show. You know for a minute it crossed my head that maybe this IDK killer was serving justice, but then the cop inside me immediately barged in saying that a crime is crime."

Ritika said, "All said, all good, but what should we do now."

Sagar said, "Salman had studied with Faisal in College, post that Imran had grown up and knew about the only two other relationships of Faisal. I think we need to go back to school."

Jitendra said, "Seriously we might not be able to crack this case, but then police academy."

Sagar and Ritika glanced at Jitendra while he said, "I am digging into the school details of Faisal, Yep Right."

This was the best bet that Team Sagar had for now. All their theories were now pointing that this ugly secret which is the reason behind these murders had some school history of Faisal. Sagar took a deep breath hoping that the days of this IDK killer would soon be over. For the first time the killer was taking credit for two murders and justice being served. Now what this justice was for was to be found, the motive behind these barbaric killings. Meanwhile the autopsy guy called Sagar.

Nitin said, "Good news detective, we have a sketch of knife, and you are going to love it."

Chapter 9

A wise man had said that good news comes to those only who are expecting it. Sagar had known that if they couldn't get hold of the murder weapon, then least they could make use of its sketch. These assets always come in handy. The autopsy team was able to make a sketch of the knife based on the pictures they took while autopsy, and the examination they had done of the wounds. The bellies of victims was a mess to examine but the autopsy people were best in their trade. This sketch was not perfect but was the closest resemblance to the knife used.

After all the hard toil one sketch was made while the other was in progress as Reshma was coordinating with the police team thoroughly. These were the moments of joy for the investigating team, however grim. Sagar was confident that the end of IDK killer was near. The pieces of puzzle were now getting together. With no CCTV footage and no Eye Witness, still Team Sagar was able to find reasonable amount of intel about this IDK killer. The only worry which was eating Sagar was that IDK killer don't strike again before getting caught. Team Sagar was sitting in their den while Nitin already had that winning smile on his face. This sketch creation was next level police work, up to parallels of best investigating agencies of the world. It was rightly said that desperate times requires desperate measures.

Sagar said, "Show me the sketch, I am already very curious."

Nitin handed him the paper, "It's a proper 12 inch kitchen knife. But the catch is that it has teeth like curves on the blunt side of the knife."

Sagar said, "I am not a very kitchen person, but is this unusual."

Nitin smiled, "Yes Detective, it's quite unusual. In fact i checked the internet and there are only 3 to 4 brands that make this model of kitchen knife, considering the knife was branded."

Sagar nodded, "And if the knife was not branded, or purchased from a conventional ironsmith."

Nitin smiled, "The chances are very low, because the remains of the steel which we found in both bodies is something that only a branded well prepared knife would leave and not that of a ironsmith. In short, it will be safe to assume that this knife was either manufactured by Kitchen Khazana, Classic Knives, Cilantro, or Pride Steel wares."

This was better than what Sagar had expected. Not just the make of knife but the brands too were sorted out by the officers. Considering this IDK killer wanted to be caught as a challenge, or least be heard, he would not have intentionally used this knife to mislead the police. Jitendra too checked the internet to corroborate the theory of Autopsy team. It was positive. He too got hit with these 4 brands. With these clues in hand, now the investigation was getting in desirable shape. It was ironical that instead of having the murder weapon, the police team had the sketch of it.

A wise man had said that whenever you feel small in the world, remember how small the world itself is. Nitin had done his job, and it was the turn of the Homicide Team to do theirs. Jitendra was pumped on making plans on how to use this Knife sketch, right when Sagar spoke out.

Sagar said, "Not yet Jitendra, it is too early to release this sketch."

Jitendra said, "Seriously Detective, what are we waiting for."

Sagar gestured a bent head to Jitendra, "Right I am gonna check with the sketch artist and Reshma."

Jitendra left while Ritika said, "Detective, what if after releasing these sketch, the killer gets alarmed and leaves the city to be never caught again. What then?"

Sagar smiled, "That risk is obvious, but least we will have no more murders. Ain't that good? Plus my gut feeling says that this IDK killer is not one of those scared criminals. He is here to do a job. I am sure he will not leave this city till he has finished what he has started."

Ritika said, "Amen to that Detective."

Meanwhile in another room in Akbar Nagar Police Station Reshma or rather Preet was holding up tight. She didn't remember the exact face but was trying her level best to give the best description. Deep down she was also little scared that if the IDK killer found out that Preet has ratted out on him, he would come after her. What else she could have expected from a serial killer. No matter what mission he was on, but he was a damn cold blooded killer whose hands didn't even trembled once while shoving that knife into the bellies of the victim. It wouldn't mean him a thing if he murdered another girl just because she acted like a roadblock in his crusade. Despite of all the assurances of the police department, Preet was scared. Sagar had got stationed two Junior Police Officers outside her residence to give cover to her family just in case if IDK killer targeted them. Preet didn't want to be a part of this, nor did she had a choice. Ironically she did had a choice when IDK killer had approached her, but her greed for few extra bucks led her to this trouble. The sketch was complete.

Sagar said, "Preet, take a good look, take a very good look and tell us if the face in this sketch is of the same person who contacted you for tricking Faisal."

Preet was confident, "Yes Detective, that is him, and the sketch without beard is the closest of what he would have looked like without beard."

Sagar nodded and turned to Jitendra, "I think we have what we need."

Ritika said, "Detective we still don't have the exact face on how he would look like without that make up. Still are you sure you want to do this."

Sagar said, "That is a chance we have to take. People should know that a serial killer is on lose and how he looks."

Sagar turned to Jitendra, "Arrange a press conference, and tell them it's a breaking news."

In all these days media was being vulture to any news regarding IDK killer. They had been broadcasting and printing regular news about the killings. To an extent that even Sagar's son Arjun knew all about the investigation without having it heard from his father. This sketch would sure go viral, this was what Sagar wanted. The only worry he had was that it better not created panic amidst people. The other worry was about wrong people getting targeted.

A wise man had said, that if you don't take chances, you will never have choices. This was a chance that Detective Sagar couldn't have missed. If this IDK killer was not a ghost, then somebody, somewhere must have seen this man. In a city of one crore, it was hard escaping the public prying eyes. This IDK killer was somewhere out there and now he needed to be scared that the Delhi Police was on to him. The terror which he has created, now needed to be bounced back to him. Conference hall of Akbar Nagar Police station was full of Journalists. They were handed down both the sketch.

Sagar said, "A warm welcome to all my media colleagues. Delhi Police has recently taken in a citizen who has seen this IDK killer. But at that time he was wearing a make up. The reason why we have forwarded you two sketches, one with beard and moustaches and one without them.. This is the closest on how this IDK killer looks like. Now Delhi Police urges you all to circulate these sketches on all your channels, and platforms. I believe that together we will be able to catch this monster."

A journalist said, "You said it is a closest match, but not exact."

Sagar said, "The reason why it is called a sketch and not a photograph of the person."

Another journalist said, "And this is the sketch of the knife which the killer used, right."

Sagar said, "That is absolutely right. We believe this knife is one of the brands of Kitchen Khazana, Classic Knives, Cilantro, or Pride Steel wares. We urge all retailers that sell the make of this knife to juggle their memory, and help us catch this killer. We have set up a hotline for any tips regarding IDK killer. We hope our citizens will cooperate."

Sagar said, "Let us catch this killer. That will be all."

Finally this weird cryptic name had got a face. IDK killer has now got an identity. As Sagar has expected, the sketch of this IDK killer was trending on all social media sites. As of this moment he was the most popular face in Delhi. If statistics were to be considered then every other person in Delhi had this sketch in their smart phones. Hypothetically it would just take a couple of days for Police to catch this killer. But Sagar knew it was tougher than that. Everything depended on how good the make up this IDK killer had used while approaching Preet.

Sagar had full trust on Preet that she had described the IDK Killer to the best of her memory, but at the same time he also had full faith on the IDK killer that he had used all his skills to mask his real face. The hotline which was set up in the

Akbar Nagar Police Station had already started buzzing. The social media account of the Delhi Police was receiving most replies on the sketch than they had received in the entire existence of the handle. Sagar was closely monitoring the hotline and the social media accounts. Meanwhile a call he was listening to went like this.

Police Officer said, "You have reached the hotline of tips on IDK killer."

The citizen said, "I am sure that I have seen the IDK Killer. He came to my shop."

Police Officer said, "Sir, are you in the business of selling kitchen knives."

The citizen said, "Yes for the past 15 years, and I am sure if you have ever visited Ashok Nagar you must have heard the name of my shop, Radhey Lal."

Police Officer said, "Sir, please describe the incidence in which you claim to have known the IDK killer."

The citizen said, "I cant forget that day, it must have been a week prior to killing of Arvind, the first victim. This man with huge beard came to my shop. He was looking confused, on which knife to pick. I helped him out, and showed the same make knife as used in murder. You know he actually tried that knife for cutting pieces of cardboard, and he did it mercilessly. Finally he bought 3 of those knives. Two he had already used and I am sure, the third he will."

Sagar gestured the police officer to drop the call. Seriously how can someone cut the pieces of cardboard mercilessly, and if yes, there should sure be a manual on this. Just like Sagar had anticipated, there were lots of call, and most of them were made by exaggerated citizens of this city. It was all routine, I mean hotlines do operate like this. In the ocean of thousands of calls you got to search for that one genuine call which can crack open the case.

A wise man had said that every man has a story to tell, but there are only few who have truly lived it. Six hours have passed by since the hotline number was announced and sketches released, but not even one single solid call came in. It wasn't like that Sagar was losing hope, as he was sure that one genuine call which he had been waiting for was just on its way. Maybe the maker of that call was buying groceries, or was busy in his office work, or was watching a cricket match, and as soon he got hold of that information he would give a call. Sagar was still actively monitoring the calls. Meanwhile another call came in, while Sagar was listening it.

Police Officer said, "You have reached the hotline of tips on IDK killer."

Citizen said, "I think I know who the IDK killer is, yes in fact I am sure about it."

Police Officer said, "Please describe the incidence where you claim to have known the IDK killer."

Citizen said, "I travel in metro every day, from home to office and office to home. But since the time when this first killing happened, I have been noticing a man during my rides. He has a huge beard and his face looks exactly like that of the killer. He never takes a seat and always stand. He always peeps around from his hoodie, like if he is trying to spot his next victim. The worst part is that after the second killing, he has been constantly watching me during my rides. I don't know why but I think I am his third victim. Please help officer."

Police Officer said, "Have you seen him carrying a knife, sir."

Citizen was baffled, "How can he carry a knife in metro after such a rigorous checking. You mean it is possible to carry a knife in metro. In that case I should be more alarmed as my life can be in more danger."

Sagar gestured the officer to cut the line and left for his cabin. Seriously how can the people of this city be so unreal. City is already down with two murders and this man on the phone is talking about how can a man carry along a knife in a metro. Sagar needed a break after listening to all those calls, a break with a cup of coffee and breath of fresh air from the window of his cabin.

A wise man had said that all good things take time, and of all those life is the best one. It always pinched Sagar when he had to investigate a murder. Sagar believed that life was the best gift any person can have and no other person in this world including Gods had the right to forfeit it. Two dead bodies were already down and Sagar was disgusted at the fact on how could a person draw blood from a dead body to leave clues. This man was a monster and before any other citizen became his victim he needed to be stopped.

What if Faisal was a womanizer who had even played dirty tricks on a girl in past, that doesn't mean he deserved to be murdered. Why would a man like Arvind deserved to die, who had no dirt in his past. This was all what had evoked disgust in Sagar against IDK Killer. Meanwhile Jitendra came in with a smile on his face.

Jitendra said, "Detective, we finally have a lead through the hotline."

Sagar said, "Don't tell me it is another tom dick or harry who had sold a knife of same make to a bearded man."

Jitendra said, "You caught it right, the beard. This lead claims that he sold a knife to a bearded person and while he was in his shop, his beard was on verge of falling off, when he adjusted it. That time the owner didn't say anything, but now after the sketches being released he is having doubts."

Sagar nodded, "Where is his shop?"

Jitendra said, "That is the best part. His shop is in Akbar Nagar."

Sagar swayed his eyes, "God, is this son of a gun from Akbar Nagar. Don't tell me."

Sagar left off his chair, to join Jitendra and Ritika in hopping on the jeep to reach that man's shop, Praveen Steel Wares. Good news are always around the corner, they just take their time. While en route, Sagar listened to the recording of the call and it did seem genuine. All the efforts of putting up a hot line had paid off. It were days like this when police work made some sense.

A wise man had said, that efforts never go in vain, sometimes they just hit at the wrong spot. Sagar was not ready to believe the possibility of this IDK killer being from Akbar Nagar. Somewhere down the line it also made some sense as both the murders had happened near or in Akbar Nagar. God, this IDK killer was doing it all while being right under the nose of Sagar. This man must have been very gutsy, to pull two murders while living in the same jurisdiction of the investigative officer. It crossed Sagar's mind, what if this IDK killer had some prior records in the Akbar Nagar Police Station. He made his mind to check on it, once he was done with this shop owner of Praveen Steel Wares. They reached the spot. It was a huge shop. Sagar recalled seeing this shop a few times while crossing the street.

Sagar said, "Thank you Mr. Praveen for calling it in. Now tell us what exactly happened."

Praveen said, "Cannot forget that incidence, this man with same face as in sketch walked in my shop. All of my workers were busy with one or the other customer, so I received him. He tells me to show the best knives I have got, the sharpest ones. He added, ones to cut the raw meats. I instantly showed him the knife from Cilantro. Its an imported brand and this customer appeared to have deep pockets. He swayed the knife on his jacket to an extent that the knife stitch a cut on it. It was very strange, but who cares it was his jacket. Then while paying me, his beard started falling off. I got suspicious, but thought he might be an actor or model. Now I get, what that beard was for."

Sagar said, "Anything you noticed about him."

Praveen said, "He wore slippers, that is the highlight. I am sure he must be from somewhere around, and he was on foot. He had a tote bag of cotton with no markings. I am afraid that's all."

Sagar thanked him while his phone rang, "Detective, the IDK killer has struck again."

Chapter 10

Ever heard of nightmares come true, for Sagar and Delhi Police this murder was a nightmare. Despite of outright efforts of Team Sagar, this murder had happened while media and people were slaughtering the image of Delhi Police. Sagar wasn't bewildered that this IDK killer would not stop. The only faith that was keeping him together was that he would nab the IDK killer before he struck, now that faith was shattered. After a very long time Sagar felt like losing to a criminal. Yep, this IDK killer has been leaving clues all this time, challenging Sagar to catch him, but Sagar failed.

With this third murder IDK killer had proven his mettle. Sagar had reached the crime scene, and there were not only policemen in plenty canvassing the crime scene but hordes of public too. Apparently Police was finding hard to control the crowd. Their curiosity was obvious. With this style of killing, this IDK killer was bound to gain popularity, and especially after the sketches made public he was enjoying the status of being a villainous celebrity. Sagar entered the spot where dead body was. It was a grotesque sight. Another man had fallen victim to this IDK killer. Sagar stood near the dead body while a Junior Police Officer approached him. Sagar was not able to take off his eyes from the dead body, and was holding himself responsible for this brutal murder.

Police Officer said, "Victim's name is Pankaj Singh. We are guessing the murder happened around 6 or 7."

Sagar said, "Any witnesses, I mean come on, in a place like this."

Police Officer shook his head, "This service lane is rarely used by anybody, the adjacent park also shares the same fate. And at this time, nobody lingers around here."

Sagar said, "Who found the body."

Police Officer said, "Few dogs started howling seeing the body, and they won't stop. A man noticed it and came by to discover the body. He is a sweeper."

Jitendra said, "Officer, any CCTV cameras around this place, I mean not necessarily at this spot."

The police officer shook his head. Again not only the Modus Operandi of this murder was same, but like always there were no witnesses. This IDK killer was good at what he did. He knew his drill. After all he had committed three murders and was still roaming free while making a mockery of the entire Delhi Police. Of all the people that were present in the crime scene, it was only Sagar who was feeling responsible for this murder. Deep down he was thinking that maybe by circulating the sketches he had just provoked this killer. But did he had another choice. This was how police functioned. The timing of this murder and the revelations were making him regret his decision.

A wise man had said, a man is guilty of all the mistakes he has made and all the mistakes he hadn't made. So true it was, Guilt was the easiest to catch infection, and no matter what Sagar would have done this murder was bound to happen. This IDK killer was not the types to deviate from his plans just because of a police pursuit. Junior Police Officer was now taking Sagar to the spot which Sagar had been eagerly waiting to see. There it was again in blood, and in huge letters.

Sagar said, "This IDK killer has got some balls. And now it is starting to annoy me."

Jitendra said, "The point is, he has done it, and I am sure he is not going to stop. I mean even this IAM doesn't completes the sentence."

Sagar said, "So AM I, not going to stop, till I catch this monster."

Ritika said, "Is he trying to establish his existence by saying IAM."

Sagar clichéd, "How could I have not guessed that he was not talking about the back of Akbar Nagar Police Station, but back of South Delhi Police Headquarters. Damn, we could have stopped this murder from happening. This murder is on us guys."

Jitendra said, "Don't be hard on yourself Detective, you had almost crack it. And who knows if the murder destination was going to be behind of Akbar Nagar Police Station, but he got alarmed to see our officers in that area, and changed his spot of murder."

This IDK killer was living up to his clues. The last one was BUT, which also got decoded by Team Sagar and here it was behind the South Delhi Police Headquarters another corpse in a bad shape. He has made it clear that he was not scared of the police. This was a direct attack on the abilities of Delhi Police. By leaving clues as big as those graffiti on the walls, he was making public participate to speculate his crimes. There were loads of posts on Social Media that have already decoded the meaning of BUT, before this murder happened which was the biggest victory of this IDK Killer.

Team Sagar was headed to meet the family of Pankaj Singh. They had already been informed, and now Sagar and his team had to do the toughest part of the job. This was the toughest part of being a policeman. Do you know why police exists, to stop such crimes from happening, and every time Sagar had to meet victims family and see it in their eyes, he knew he had failed. Pankaj lived near the South Delhi Police Headquarters, which meant that getting him to the murder spot must not have been onerous. They have reached his house, where a huge crowd had already gathered to pay their regards. The only uninvited people and seen with hostility were Team Sagar. They soon sat with the wife of Pankaj Singh, Priyanka who was clearly looking broken.

Sagar said, "We are sorry for your loss, but would just like to ask few questions. We will make it quick."

Priyanka said, "Are you really sorry, or just incompetent of catching a murderer. You knew he was going to strike again, but you did nothing. If asking me questions can really help you catch this IDK killer, I would be the first one to answer them"

Sagar said, "Did somebody took Pankaj out, or was he going to meet someone."

Priyanka said, "He was returning from Office when he called me and told me that he had bumped into an old friend, and will be late for home."

Sagar said, "Did he gave a name, or any detail about that friend."

Priyanka said, "I asked Pankaj who was this friend, but he would not say. He just hinted, it was somebody from his past and I didn't know him. For me it was all normal. I didn't knew he was going to be murdered, or I would have sure asked some more questions."

Priyanka left, while Team Sagar was offered tea to drink. It was making sense on why else Pankaj would walk down to a deserted piece of land behind Police Headquarters without knowing a person, but could this IDK killer be a friend of Pankaj from past. It was a sensible guess supported by facts, as someone who had known Pankaj over the years could have built this rage against him to an extent of murdering him. Maybe Pankaj was meeting with an old friend and when that old friend took off, this IDK killer jumped in.

Like all of his victims, this IDK killer must have been keeping an eye on Pankaj, and when he got the chance he pounced on. This was how criminals work, especially murderers who wait for their victims to be alone and vulnerable. For now Sagar was sure feeling alone, in the house of Pankaj. He was constantly being stared by the family members. Meanwhile father of Pankaj, Prakash came in. He greeted Team Sagar and sat beside them. It was sad to see an old man lose his son, but this was life. Sagar didn't even made an eye contact with him.

Prakash said, "There is something that might help you people in catching that criminal."

Sagar turned back to Prakash, "Please, anything you know that might help."

Prakash sighed, "You know since the first murder of that chap, uh, Arvind, my son has been closely following the news of this IDK killer. Many a times I thought about asking him why was he showing so much interest in these killings, but I didn't. After the second murder of Faisal, it felt he was pretty disturbed to see him die."

Sagar said, "Are you implying that your son knew these two people."

Prakash shrugged, "I wished I had talked to my son about this, but now I can only assume."

Sagar's ears have longed much to hear this, and after all he was right that these three people knew each other. It couldn't have been possible that this IDK killer was so maniac that he was picking his victims randomly. The only melancholy that Sagar had was of being late, or rather Prakash was a bit late. It also meant that maybe Pankaj knew that he was going to be murdered. But then why didn't he approached the police, or least he could have been more careful. In that case if Pankaj knew that he was going to be killed, he would have never gone with that friend his wife was talking about unless he felt completely safe with this friend. The worst case scenario would be that Pankaj knew that he was about to get killed, and just wanted to sort out the differences with this IDK killer whom he referred to as a friend to his wife.

It was very important who this friend was as it held the key to cracking this case. Team Sagar was headed out of the house of Pankaj, and soon they were sitting in their den watching news on this new victim of IDK killer. A police officer from IT team came inside.

Sagar said, "Any leads from his phone records."

IT officer said, "Nothing detective, nothing from the day that could raise a brow."

IT officer left while Jitendra said, "As per Priyanka, Pankaj had called her when he had hopped off the metro station. Maybe we should check near the metro station, if someone had spotted him with another man."

Ritika hopped in, "That area is quite deserted, and I am sure we wont find any CCTV cameras there. I have checked with the Delhi Metro Office, their cameras on the gates of Metro station had been dysfunctional for quite many days. Apparently they are waiting for the funds to be released to fix it."

Sagar nodded, "I think it's a good idea to check with the locals from outside the metro station, let's go."

In a world of smart phones and internet, Team Sagar was going on a manual hunt. If someone was to ask them, they didn't have any choice. Finding this mystery friend from the past had now become paramount. Deep in his heart Sagar was praying that it better be a good old friend rather than the IDK killer. The reason being, if this was IDK killer, then some real ugly secret has been hiding all this long.

The car got stopped near the gates of metro station while Jitendra and Ritika hopped down to ask the locals if they had spotted Pankaj, with any other man. Most of these conversations were dead ends. They refused before even seeing the picture. The relief was that Team Sagar didn't expected a lot from this ask the locals. Sagar knew the drill, but just like the Hotline success, he was sure that someone with prying eyes must recall Pankaj from the other night. The hunt went on while Sagar also joined. After walking for a bit, they spotted a small stall selling mobile covers. This wasn't odd, but what caught their eyes was that the owner of this stall was constantly watching people waking on the street while he tried hard selling his mobile accessories to the people. Sagar crossed his finger while they approached him.

Jitendra said, "Hey, do you have license to sell these mobile covers here."

The stall owner was scared, "Sir I am poor man, please do not charge me with fine. I pay weekly fee to the police officer in charge of the area."

Sagar came in and said, "No worries, but you will have to help us. Did you see this man, yesterday."

The stall owner came in closer to see the picture and with gleam said, "100 percent sir, he walked out of gate no. 3, and has walked by my stall. I even tried selling him my covers, to which he gently shook the head. But he was not alone, a big man with large beard, and a hoodie was walking with him. They were having friendly chat."

Team Sagar glanced each other, while Jitendra said, "Hey don't you follow news. That hoodie man could be the IDK Killer, the sketch we have circulated on internet and in media."

The stall owner said, "You are right sir, he looked like the sketch. I saw it too."

Team Sagar left the stall. The path where this stall was led to the back side of South Delhi Police Headquarters.. Team Sagar was now positive that they must have walked down this path and as soon as they had reached the murder spot the IDK Killer must have executed his act. But in all of this, why would Pankaj walk with a man that fits the description of IDK killer. Pankaj was closely following the news, and must have seen that sketch, and as per assumption Pankaj also knew that his life was in danger, then why such stupidity.

This was not making sense. They have turned on their torches and were walking on that path, while closely watching the surroundings. They were hoping if they would catch a sight of a CCTV camera, or maybe some other clue that Pankaj might have dropped. They walked and walked, but the path was as deserted as its reputation. The only thing that caught their attention was the stinking poop of stray animals. How could Pankaj be that stupid, or maybe this IDK killer was way more manipulative than the Police had perceived. Team Sagar was standing at the crime scene which still had a police officer guarding it.

Jitendra said, "It doesn't make any sense, on why would Pankaj walk with the IDK killer in same appearance as we warned the public about."

Sagar said, "Maybe this IDK killer told Pankaj that he was ready to surrender and walks him to the PH."

Ritika nodded, "That is the closest explanation I can think of."

Jitendra said, "But from what I have heard, Pankaj was not that stupid of a man. I mean even if this IDK killer had proposed him that he would surrender, he was not that stupid to walk with him on that deserted path. You know detective it has just crossed my mind, on what if Pankaj had left us some clue after he realized that it was just a trap. He could have done that. And this is the image I have of him."

Ritika said, "But haven't we walked the entire path, but found nothing."

Sagar nodded, "I think we should check his phone again."

They glanced at each other, while they got headed back to the Akbar Nagar Police Station. Now this investigation was dependent on the assumption if Pankaj was that smart to leave behind a trace in case if anything dreadful happened to him. Jitendra was right in his place. Pankaj might not have been a heavy weight champion, but he worked for an IT company and certainly had that kind of brain. No one was judging his IQ, but he must have done something the moment he would have realized that his life was going to meet a dreadful end.

Team Sagar was sitting in the IT cell while officers were making a copy of his cell phone in their computer. They were now tracking every small detail of activity done on the mobile phone. Thankfully it was a smart phone so the trouble was less. All the activity log of Pankaj's smart phone was on the screen. Wait, what was that, a new sticky note creation. The IT team opened the note that was created right around the time of murder. Pankaj must have written something that he wanted to be found out.

Jitendra read loud, "I am with IDK, chec Saint Mary's. Phew that is something."

Ritika said, "He had miss spelled check, must be in a hurry."

Sagar said, "Isn't that a school near Pankaj's house. It could be his alma mater."

Ritika said, "Whatever it is, Pankaj must have been sure that we will find something over there. Or else he wouldn't have written it. Actually it makes sense, as the time when Pankaj must have been in school, would be long back."

Sagar said, "I have the same feeling, as Faisal's investigation also referred to some time before college."

Jitendra said, "Lets wait till the new day begins."

Team Sagar had got their big lead, and it was now proven that Pankaj had quite a high IQ. Team Sagar wasn't sure on what explanation he might have given to IDK killer while using the Phone. Now the next stop was St. Mary's.

Chapter 11

A wise man had said that everybody dies, but not everybody lives. It was time for Team Sagar to find out what life Pankaj had at St. Mary's. It was now no secret that a secret had been hiding, a secret so profound that had driven this IDK killer to murder three people. Jitendra had already confirmed it with Prakash that yes Pankaj had studied in Saint Mary. Sagar was more than ever curious on what could Pankaj had done when he was a kid to drive this madness into the city. Maybe bully someone that was the closest guess anybody could make.

The only thing that Sagar worried was if he will be able to find anything from St. Mary's before IDK struck again. It had been a long time since Pankaj had studied there, so chances of finding the truth were slim. Most of the students from his batch would have been by now scattered throughout the country, and the teachers who taught him by now must have retired. But still it were the last words of Pankaj to check St. Mary's and it must have a real connection to this case or else Pankaj wouldn't have wasted his last words on it. Sagar was inside the school, nostalgia hit him hard that made him remember his own school days. Seriously school days were the best days of any person. He sat with the principal.

Sagar said, "I know it is a very odd request, considering the student we are inquiring about was a pass out decades ago. But did you found anything on Pankaj."

Principal smiled, "Detective, anything to catch that IDK Killer, more importantly anything to catch the killer of Pankaj who was once our student. You might not know, but ever since the inception of this school we have been maintaining a disciplinary committee. Which means any mischief, or any bad act by student is seen by this committee, and we also keep a record of it. I checked, in fact I double checked, but nothing on Pankaj."

Sagar said, "So you mean he was one of those good kids, with no beef with anyone and no sin."

Principal said, "Well, every kid does some mischief or other, but Pankaj didn't do a thing that could raise a brow. Yes he was a good kid with consistent good grades in his classes."

Sagar exhaled, "Okay what about our request of talking with someone who might have taught him."

Principal smiled, "It's been honored. In fact you are lucky that we have a teacher from that era."

Good grades, and no naughty acts, was all pointing towards the fact that hardly Pankaj could have been a bully, or would have done something that profound to create a monster like IDK killer.

A wise man had said, facts can be misleading, as nobody knows the facts of the person who created them. Sagar didn't want to leave any room for error. If Pankaj had said, check in St. Mary's then there has to be something in here. Maybe one of his acts went un noticed by the disciplinary committee. It happens all the time, kids cover up their mistakes by scaring other kids to not go to the authorities.

They were headed to meet the Mathematics teacher, Mr. Basu who also had been the Mathematics teacher of Pankaj when he studied here. It was long time ago, but Mr. Basu still remembered Pankaj as per what Principal had told Sagar. They were crossing the alleys besides classroom. The chit chatter of kids was bringing back joy to Sagar. At the same moment he thought if he had told Sarika that he went to a school for investigation, then another fight would erupt. The last time Sagar spoke to any teacher or principal of Arjun's school was when he was a toddler. Soon they stood outside the classroom of Mr. Basu who was busy teaching kids. Principal knocked at the door and seeing them Mr. Basu smiled and walked out.

Sagar said, "Thank you Mr. Basu, for speaking with us. Now tell us everything you remember about Pankaj."

Mr. Basu wiped his glasses with napkin, "That kid was a genius, always used to top in Mathematics. While I taught his class, he was one of my favorite students. It is very sad that someone killed him, though when I saw it on news, I couldn't match him to the boy I taught, after all he looked so grown up."

Sagar said, "Did he used to bully kids, or girls of the class. Or any naughty act as a kid."

Mr. Basu said, "Not him, but one of his best friends Rohan Singh sure used to bully kids. He was rather a joyful person. I know what you are suggesting, but I don't think that is the case in here."

Sagar nodded, "Tell me more about his friends."

Mr. Basu smiled, "I already have. What I mean is, Rohan was his only best friend, though he was on talking terms with all of the class, but if you are seeking any secrets, then better catch up with Rohan."

Sagar had got what he wanted, a name of a secret keeper of Pankaj, or what in normal language we call best friends. Before leaving the school, Sagar even dug out the details of Rohan. Sagar didn't get a breakthrough by coming to St. Mary, but he did get another name. If Pankaj was right, and he sure was that something had been hiding in St. Mary, then Rohan would know it.

Sagar still was not able to understand how Pankaj, Arvind and Faisal were connected. Maybe Rohan knew their relationship. This was all very overwhelming, meanwhile Sagar was already scared on how soon was this IDK killer was going to strike again. He had left another clue already, IAM, and sure it was the next location of the murder. But who was now going to be the target was still a mystery. If Sagar was able to crack this St. Mary connection he would sure be able to stop this IDK Killer. Team Sagar was already headed to the Akbar Nagar Police Station. Sagar had been called as the autopsy of Pankaj was done, and Sagar couldn't have waited to know the report. He was standing with the Autopsy guy Nitin. Sagar was hopeful that Nitin came out some more revealing facts.

Nitin said, "The MO is same, so is the murder weapon. Yes the same knife was used to kill Pankaj too."

Nitin continued, "But this time something odd has happened, which caught my attention and I am sure that it will catch your attention too."

Sagar curiously said, "I am all ears Nitin."

Nitin smiled, "Arvind was stabbed 9 times, then Faisal was stabbed 10 times, and in that equation Pankaj should have been stabbed 11 times. But no, Pankaj was stabbed again 9 times."

Sagar said, "That could have been the only mistake by this IDK killer, maybe while stabbing Faisal he miss counted his number of blows."

Nitin nodded, "Everyone would think like that, but here is the catch. These blows of stabs are full blows, which means every time this IDK killer has stabbed, he has completely inserted the knife in victims belly. With such patient blows, I hardly think that he must have miss counted. I think just like his clues, he is trying to communicate something, through a pattern."

Sagar nodded, as Nitin was making sense. Could 9, 10, 9 mean ups and downs, it was hard to say, as this killer was communicating a lot of things. For now Nitin left. Sagar was now left to think what this IDK killer was trying to convey with the number of blows. He was hiding from police, then why was he leaving clues. He could have directly written on the wall with same blood the reason why he was killing all these people. Maybe he was scared if he told the entire truth up front, he would not be able to kill all the people he think or might they have done something wrong with him.

He was buying some time. But then again why all this long gap between the murders. Maybe he was little scared of being hasty and being caught. One thing was sure that him leaving the clues were part of plan to show the world that he was serving justice and all these people deserved to die. He was treating the people as jury to see his acts, and figure out why he was committing all these murders. Team Sagar was sitting in their den and there was only one thing in their minds, the IDK killer.

Jitendra said, "We know that this IDK killer will strike again, but again we don't know when where who."

Ritika said, "It only implies that we are failing in our jobs."

Sagar said, "Hey guys, do not lose your confidence, this is what this IDK killer wants. We have to believe that we can catch him, it is only then when are going to catch him. It might sound a little hard, but we got to catch him before he is finished. We are dealing with a very smart criminal and we got to give our best."

Jitendra said, "I doubt, but did he knew that CCTV outside the metro station was not working. If yes, then someone is ratting us out."

Sagar exhaled, "That is a very big window to find out, and we need to stick to the primary clues, okay. Now let's call upon that linguistic expert of ours, and see what now this IAM means."

With three dead bodies down, and three clues on board, this investigation had completely become a game of cat and mouse. People were scared but they were also enjoying this dark game of can you catch me. Media was brutally murdering the reputation of police while claiming that this IDK killer was some product of great injustice. Everyone had something to gossip about this IDK killer. He was the new hot topic of discussion.

A wise man had said, if a criminal becomes popular, then first bring down his popularity before catching him. Sagar knew this, and he never missed an opportunity to come up in front of camera and call this killer a monster, but the odds were against him. Now only when he would find the motive behind these serial killings he would get a chance to destroy the reputation of this IDK killer. Meanwhile the young police officer who had masters in English, and was designated to crack these clues has already arrived in Sagar's cabin. It was the first time that Sagar was meeting him. He looked confident and had already expressed his gratitude of being given this task. He was a junior police officer but working on such a hyped investigation was giving him goose bumps and a greater sense of satisfaction. Team Sagar sat while the young police officer took the charge.

Puneet said, "We will come back later to the sentence, but first let's talk about what IAM means for us."

Puneet continued, "As we all know that this killer is sending us clues in form of a location. Considering that our next location should be very iconic, iconic in eyes of the people, or iconic in terms of his life or his growing years. Don't think he is calling us to his home directly, but."

Jitendra interrupted, "Hey I am not interested in the theory, tell me the location."

Puneet smiled, "Considering all the murders are happening in South Delhi, I believe the Victory park could be a match, not just because it is iconic, but also because it has a sculpture with I Heart Delhi. This is my first guess. My second guess would be UIDAI Headquarters which is the Aadhar Card Head Quarters, again in South Delhi. Maybe he is trying to say, that I am not in your records. My guess is he has a Aadhar Card, but not in your Police Records. My third guess is St. Mary, yes Ritika told me about that. I mean school is the first place where kids get the identity card. I am sure if this killer is from the same school, he will use some deserted lane around it."

Sagar said, "These are too many guesses at one, tell me your top pick, one or two."

Puneet rolled his tongue to his teeth, "Victory Park, or someplace near to where he used to live or lives."

Victory Park was pleasure to be heard as it was quite a place which could have been secured by the diligent policemen of Delhi least for a week or so, but then how was Sagar supposed to know what locality he used to live or lives. But again this could also have been a blessing in disguise. If the killer was revealing his address, then what could have been better. Chances of finding this monster would only narrow down but at a cost of another disaster.

A wise man had said, that a person never invites you to his home without any reason. It was true, even the family is invited to share happiness, or grief, or anything important to discuss. If this killer was inviting Delhi Police to his home, then sure he must have been planning to also reveal the motive of these murders. This could be one of the possibility, because by doing so he would gain public sympathy, and get a chance to walk out of these crimes. The police was never going to walk him away, but you know how sentimental people are.

This revelation was quite a hope after a long, but still Sagar was worried, because if this murder was to happen near his place, then Sagar would not be able to stop it. Puneet continued with his findings about the completion of the sentence.

Puneet said, "As I see, the next murder which he is planning is either the end of it, or start of really something long. But my guts say that this could be the end."

Sagar said, "I am all years Puneet, tell me what could be the next clue, or completion of this sentence."

Puneet said, "I am not sure, but maybe MAD, as we still are not unable to connect the victims. Plus I am considering that in here too he will use a 3 character word. Maybe a single word, or maybe an acronym."

Sagar said, "3 Characters I get it, but anything else than mad."

Puneet said, "With reference to all the material I have read, I infer that some woman angle is there in this murder. So my next guess is little cheeky, but quite passionate. ILU, I love you. Could be a great possibility that he is gonna paint ILU. Now in reference to the same woman, in case if she is already dead, then the next clue could also be IMU, I miss you. Maybe the death of this woman was because of our 3 victims."

Sagar exhaled, "Hey that is enough for now, but keep working, we will keep you in loop."

This was overwhelming and a little confusing at the same time. Instead of making Sagar's work easy, Puneet has just pushed in so many ideas into his head. But it did made sense. Sagar was considering strengthening the police force near Victory Park. The two sides of this park had deserted areas around, and probably that could have been the best spot for IDK Killer to strike again. All Sagar was hoping was that he able to catch this killer before 4th dead body fell down. It was cringe worthy that all his life Sagar had cracked the toughest of criminals, but it was only in this instance that he failed to do so.

Was Sagar really getting old to have taken up a desk job rather than a field job, this question was haunting him and continuously hammering his conscious. After all, these three deaths in the jurisdiction of Sagar meant that Sagar was responsible for these deaths. He hadn't been able to maintain safety of citizens in his jurisdiction. Team Sagar sat with cup of freshly made coffee. They were now reading the report of this guy Puneet. Despite of being a policeman he sure knew the drill around English.

Jitendra said, "ILU, I mean how could Puneet even think about this possibility. This is the cheekiest thing that a Criminal would say. If IDK killer was a teenager then too he would not write that considering the gravity of his acts. This guess is total crap, how am I supposed to believe it and then plan my investigation around it."

Ritika said, "But what if this IDK killer is a teenager. You know they are smart, and intelligent."

Sagar said, "She is right, if this IDK killer can use a teenager acronym IDK, then I can bet on any night, he can also use this ILU, or maybe even IMU."

Sagar said, "You know it makes sense, if the mystery woman we are thinking as the reason of this investigation is already dead, because only a death can invoke such passion and brutality at the same time."

Jitendra said, "If you both are true, then this killer ought to be her son."

Sagar said, "I do not deny the possibility, but as you speak of a son, I think I need a home break."

Jitendra and Ritika smiled, while Sagar left for his home. Apart from saving the city from criminals, he also had a responsibility of running a house. A son and a wife were two people apart from this IDK killer that were hoping to be caught up with. Sagar knew that he would either get a huge lashing from his wife or a complete silence. Sarika was too predictable in such circumstances, or one could say that she had only two weapons, or a cop could say that she had the same Modus Operandi.

Sagar was driving, he saw an ice cream parlor open, and damn it was a good idea to buy some to break the ice in home. A wise man had said that a family can kill the greatest of grief. He was so right, as Sagar was already feeling relaxed. Sagar turned his hand to see the watch, and was sure that she must have made it to home by now. His phone rang, and it was Ishwar Das Kashyap, not God.

Ishwar Das said, "Detective I have something important to discuss about IDK killer, i hope we can meet tomorrow."

Chapter 12

A wise man had said, that there is only one thing without which the world would cease to exist and that is family. Sagar always felt guilty whenever he was unable to give his time to his family. The reason was that Sagar under took every investigation as sincerely as that of this IDK killer. Till there were criminals roaming free in this city, and Sagar had a badge on his chest, this guilt was just bound to only soar. In the end of the day, what mattered was that Sagar loved his job. It was not just the perks of wearing a uniform or driving an official car with siren, or juniors saluting every time he passed by. But the sheer happiness Sagar got while catching a criminal was the reason behind his hustle.

Sagar always believed if cops took their jobs seriously, no one would have to die, no one would have to be robbed, and no one had to be scammed. For now, this call of Ishwar had certainly piqued Sagar's interest to an extent that he wanted to drive on till he stopped at Ishwar's house, but he couldn't stop the father inside him and he couldn't stop the husband inside him. Sagar was at the doorstep and wished that Sarika be in good mood. Her eyes were also a killer whenever Sagar missed a day or two coming back home. To his surprise Arjun opened the door, with a huge smile on his face.

Sagar said, "Hey champ, how you doing. Missed you a lot"

Arjun said, "I know third dead body has fallen down, so I wont complain, as catching this IDK killer is hell more important than being present at dinner table."

Sagar said, "Stop watching these stupid news channels, in your age I was completely hooked to cartoons and sports. You should try it too."

Arjun said, "Dad that is because there were no smart phones back then."

Sagar smiled while Sarika interrupted, "And also because fathers did their duties way well."

Sagar waved his head, "Is there any dinner left behind or should I order something."

Sarika smiled sarcastically and went inside, while Sagar felt the chills of disappointment. All the enthusiasm he had while coming to his own place was now all vanished. He had expected to eat dinner with Arjun and share the silence with Sarika. But forget eating alone, there wasn't even food made for Sagar. This was rather hostile, but then Sagar had no rights to complain about this, as he was out on his job for past 2 days and including 2 nights. Sagar cozily sat to turn on the television but again it was all flooded with stories on IDK killer. Sagar was least interested to know what media was thinking about this investigation, as all they thought was produced out of TRP machine.

The food Sagar had ordered had been delivered, and consciously he had also ordered some ice cream for Arjun, knowing that Sarika could get mad seeing him destroy his teeth. But who cared, this was father son thing. Sagar was enjoying his Fried Chicken while Arjun was eating his ice cream, as they both watched a recorded cricked match being played on television. Sarika entered and switched off the lights, and gestured to Arjun that it was time to doze off. First food and now this ban on television.. Sagar entered the bed room.

Sarika had already placed the papers for boarding school on bed, seeing them Sagar felt a jolt of disappointment. He said, "Don't tell me that you have already enrolled him."

Sarika said, "If you had been missing from home for another 2 or 3 days, I certainly would have."

Sagar said, "What is your problem, I really do not get it."

Sarika turned with an angry face, "How could you even say that, what is my problem. It is you who goes missing from home for 2 3 4 5 or even a week in one instance. It is you who is a no show at his school, it is you who do a dangerous job to an extent that we have been threatened of life twice. It is you who doesn't even have time to pick Arjun or drop Arjun to the school, the least. And you are asking what is my problem."

Sagar said, "Fine, do as you wish, I won't complain a thing."

IDK Killer that too right now, Sagar's head was saying to this IDK killer to go to hell. Maybe he shouldn't have even come home to listen such a distressing decision of Sarika. But eventually she was right at her place. Sarika was always very serious about her career and she had made it clear even before they got married. It was Sagar who has dragged her to this day to day chores while he was busy chasing his passion or rather say putting bad guys in prison. This day had to come, while Sagar had only hoped that Arjun be all grown up to have not even needed a boarding school.

Sagar knew that he was barely home, even if then only to sleep in his cozy bed, but then the thought of Arjun not being in his room which was only few feet away was scary. Now Sagar would get only weekends to meet his son. Thankfully the boarding school that Sarika had selected was in Delhi, this was the only good part of her decision. The entire night Sagar couldn't sleep well on thoughts of his son being all alone in a dormitory. Soon the sun had risen and Sagar was still in bed trying to catch up with all those sleepless nights. He got awakened by a gentle push of his son.

Arjun said, "Are Boarding schools cool, because I am getting a strange feeling about it."

Sagar smiled, "I do not know if they are cool or not, but even I am getting a strange feeling about it."

Arjun said, "Mom says it is good for my future. She says I will become a much stronger person when I will walk out of that school. Plus once I am a teenager, I can return back to home, but wouldn't that be a time of me heading to college. I think it is my time for goodbye to home."

Sagar clichéd, "Do not worry, if you don't like that boarding school, you just have to tell me, and I will get you out of there. Its all covered, don't worry a thing Champ."

Arjun frowned his face, "I hope you will come to meet me."

Sagar said, "Needless to say, and why you are acting like that you are just going there. We still have some time together, so you better enjoy all of these moments."

Sagar patted on his back while he went to freshen up. This IDK killer who had gone to hell the other night was now back. Sagar was curious on what did Ishwar had to say, when he clearly stated that he didn't knew Arvind. Wait, maybe he had known Faisal or Pankaj. Anyways, this old man surely had something solid, or he would have never ringed Sagar. Sagar was already racing his car towards the Akbar Nagar Police Station. All those harrowing thoughts about his son going to boarding school started haunting his head. I mean was Boarding school any less than a prison. Sagar thought so, after being confined to a campus, with nowhere else to go till you had your guardian's presence. It was now he was realizing that his job was snatching away his joys of being with his son.

Was this police job more important than being with his son. Of all the questions, this was the one whom Sagar didn't have answer to. Maybe Sagar kept his mind numb and distracted when ever this question popped up. Maybe he was trying to escape the truth. He had reached the police station with Jitendra and Ritika already waiting for him. In his cabin was sitting Ishwar. Sagar entered with a smile.

Sagar said, "Thanks for the cooperation Sir, I really appreciate it you all coming to this place to help us. Now tell me, what is it about IDK killer you know."

Ishwar smiled, "Back then when you asked me about Arvind, I refused, because really I never knew him. But then last evening I was watching a news channel, it had the families of all the victims of IDK killer. IT was then I recognized a face that was familiar from my past."

Sagar said, "And who was it."

Ishwar sighed, "It was Ashima. In fact I know her entire family. See when I used to live in that locality I was a budding journalist who also took freelance work to meet my ends. I still remember that day when Ashima's father came to me to offer me a gig to take pictures of wedding celebrations ceremony in their house. See that was only on the side of bride, so I never got to see Arvind, in fact I could have, as Ashima's father had also asked me to capture pictures in wedding too, but I had some other commitments so I refused."

Sagar said, "Do you think it's a coincidence that initials of your names are IDK."

Ishwar came closer, "I know there is a woman angle in this investigation, and trust me that angle now also includes a marriage, a failed one or a widowed one, that you have to find out."

A wise man had said that all things unexpected are mostly good. It was moment for Sagar to realize it. Sagar had even forgotten Ishwar, but here he was with a connection to this IDK killer, or rather say connection to one of IDK killer victim. This IDK killer surely had lot to say, and he was using these three characters to the best of capacity. It was official that this IDK killer also meant IDK for Ishwar Das Kashyap. If that was true then BUT standing for Salman Butt was also true. Both these connections were suggesting that maybe these three victims broke a marriage, or caused a huge trouble in a woman's life.

This was all just a theory, but a very concrete one. Sagar knew that this could lead to the catching of this killer, as now he almost knew the motive. This IDK being Ishwar Das Kashyap was no coincidence, especially when Salman Butt had shown up in their police station. This puzzle was finally making sense, but now the biggest question was who was this woman, to whom these three victims had done wrong..This was eating up away Sagar like anything. It was a feeling of being this close like standing just on the edge of a cliff. All Sagar needed was a hand in form of another lead which could make him nab this killer. Team Sagar sat with a cup of coffee. Everyone was in awe of the new lead that they have uncovered.

Jitendra said, "A photographer from the wedding of victim number one. Is it just this, or do we need to dig deeper. He could have conveyed this very easily through anything else."

Ritika said, "I agree, there is more to it. Think we should look into this."

Sagar nodded, "What if there is a person who knows all of this, just like Ishwar, or just like Salman."

Jitendra held his head, "Detective, that has to be, why didn't it crossed my mind."

Ritika said, "Someone like an eye witness who saw the injustice done to that woman. But if any such person is alive, then why isn't he coming in front after hearing that three people have already died. Was the sin too dark that was done to this woman that this person sees these murders as justice being served."

Sagar waved his head, "You are on point, but first we got to juggle what we have. Find Rohan"

The pieces of this murder were now speaking for themselves. Team Sagar was finally getting to the bottom of this investigation, but the unfortunate part was that this IDK killer was still on loose. Even after circulating the sketch of this killer, he was able to abduct his another victim Pankaj from a public place that too in the same get up. This only showed that how badly Police has failed.

The next best lead that Team Sagar had was Rohan, and they couldn't have missed this one. Maybe Rohan was that eye witness, or the one person who knew everything about the sin of Arvind, Pankaj, and Faisal. The travesty of this investigation was that Team Sagar was still not able to figure out the connection between these three victims. Not even a single lead or a clue that could connect them all. Maybe in injustice towards this woman there was a part played by all these three. But if according to present evidences it was established that this happened sometime when they were in school, then weren't they too young to destroy any woman.

Jitendra had got back with a search on Rohan. He had sent a police officer to Rohan's home.

Jitendra said, "Its not a good news detective, but still we can do something good about it."

Sagar said, "Stop being this cryptic, we already have this IDK killer to do that job. Anyways, I am getting used to bad news in this investigation, so just shoot up."

Jitendra said, "Rohan no longer lives in India. He has a job in California, and has been living there for past 5 years."

Ritika chuckled, "And the good news is that you can probably arrange a video call with our Rohan. You know what Jitendra, you would have sucked if you were that IDK killer, your clues are too predictive."

Jitendra frowned while Sagar said, "Okay let us do it that way, because in any case we need to talk to him."

It might not have been evident, but Sagar was already fearing it that Rohan might not be living in Delhi as a possibility. But he didn't expected to meet this Rohan especially on a video call. In Police line the physical presence is of utmost importance. The gestures, the body language, the reactions are most important part of questioning. Jitendra contacted Rohan who was now waking up back in California while it was already evening in India. Apparently Rohan's parents had already informed him, and it came to him like a shock that Pankaj was murdered, and as a best friend once upon a time he was all hands to help the police in any possible way.

A wise cop had said, that never mess with a man who has too many friends. Sagar was hoping hard that Rohan turned out to be as best of a friend as Mr Basu had hinted.. It was no surprise to Sagar that with time everything changes. It might have been possibility that Rohan had forgotten everything about Pankaj, but what mattered was if he remembered the secrets that Pankaj might have trusted him with. The call was made, while the video calling software was tuned to record the statement of Rohan. He had a grieving face, and probably hadn't slept since he came to know about Pankaj's murder.

Sagar said, "Thanks Rohan, for doing this. It means a lot, and trust me, we will get Justice for Pankaj."

Rohan exhaled, "I still can't believe it that someone murdered him. He was one of the most positive people I had ever known. Detective, I am a very selfish man, and I always struggled in making friends. But Pankaj was always there for me. Anything for my friend"

Sagar nodded, "Be strong Rohan. Now as per our investigation we believe that Pankaj, Arvind, and Faisal, the three victims, have done something wrong to a woman, and we believe this must have happened when Pankaj was in school. Does it ring any bell."

Rohan said, "For past two hours I have been catching up with news about this IDK killer. And truly I don't recall any of these two names, Faisal and Arvind. But Pankaj was not that kind of guy. There is something I want to tell you that Pankaj wished he had told me."

Sagar was all ears, while Rohan said, "I still remember we had just graduated from our schools, and it was after the last board exams, that we were having drinks together. I was set to leave Delhi to join a college in Chennai. In fact many times I asked Pankaj to come with me, his scores were good and he would have got admission in my college too, but he wanted to stay in Delhi with his parents. Anyways, we were having drinks and we didn't knew after how long were we going to meet. It was then he told me, that Rohan I have done something very bad, and I don't think god is ever going to forgive me. It shook me and I asked what had he done, but he wont say. I don't know why but I think it is that act of Pankaj that has got him murdered."

Sagar sighed, "That was helpful Rohan, and we might connect with you again."

I have done something very bad, now it seemed like if Pankaj and the other two victims might have murdered somebody. Who talks like that. This investigation was now unfolding its ugly layers. What appeared like some bullying to which this Psycho IDK Killer might have taken to his heart was now turning out to be a deadly secret. What have these three kids done that they were so ashamed of disclosing. Neither Faisal talked about it, nor did Pankaj, and all they hinted was that they have done something very bad.

Rohan might not have helped in getting closer to killer, but sure he had strengthened the belief of Team Sagar. Team Sagar had got back in to their den from the conference room and there was a weird silence in between them. As if somewhere they felt that IDK killer might have been doing a great job. A police officer came striding into their cabin. Sagar crossed his finger hoping that IDK killer had not struck again.

The Police Officer said, "Detective, Rajeev wants to speak. He says he might have something on the killer."

Chapter 13

A wise man had said that not every flower has fragrance but they do have colors of their own. This IDK killer might have done these murders out of vengeance but still he was a criminal. No place in this world was justified to take a life if you lost one. Team Sagar was headed to meet Rajeev, the same old wretched friend of Arvind, the same old selfish friend who didn't spared the opportunity to make some money out of a murdered Arvind. He was not charged with fraud and had even returned the money to Ashima. It was exactly like what Sagar had anticipated. You know how lawyers are, and Rajeev had got himself a very good one.

It must have been guilt that was haunting Rajeev, or else why would he volunteer up to giving leads to Sagar for the murder of his so called friend. He must have realized that even though he didn't considered Arvind as a friend but just a goat to sacrifice, Arvind did had friendly feelings for him. How strange it was that we live our lives thinking that we have friends, we have best friends, but when the time comes it all looks like a camouflage. Team Sagar was sitting in the home of Rajeev, who had a bleak smile on his face. Maybe that was his gesture to pretend nice and innocent.

Sagar said, "I heard you wanted to help us."

Rajeev said, "You heard that right detective. Since I have been acquitted by court, I have had sleepless nights. I just cannot forget the face of Arvind. He has always been nice to me despite of things I did to him. I think now is the time to be a good friend, and get him justice."

Jitendra said, "Tell us something we don't know, or cannot anticipate."

Rajeev took a sip of tea and said, "Like I said at that time too, I wasn't going to fraud Arvind, it was just turn of events. In fact I was about to put all his money into a Pharma firm, Star Medicals. But it was not just it. Before meeting with Arvind, a week back I received an anonymous mail that claimed that stock prices of Star Medicos was going to hit all time high, as they were in process of launching some novel medicines for cancer. It piqued my interest and when I investigated, it came out to be true. Now somehow I think that it wasn't just an anonymous tipper, but that mail came from IDK killer."

Sagar said, "We will need your laptop, the device on which you received the mail, and thanks for doing the right thing."

Rajeev said, "Oh I had figured it out, it is right there. Just catch this man detective."

Sagar reciprocated the same bleak smile and left. Rajeev was doing the right thing, even though Sagar didn't say it on his face. Maybe it was just a horrid mistake that Rajeev committed by scamming the family of Arvind. In all these years of police work, Sagar had very well known how easily devil can play with your mind by attracting you to do all sinister things. After all Rajeev was also just a man, a vulnerable man who had that opportunity.

Now what Rajeev had said had piqued the attention of Sagar. Sagar didn't expected any miracles from chasing this lead, but still he wanted to give it a try. Deep down in his heart he feared what if Star Medicals would also turn out to be a dead end. This IDK killer was smart and could have easily bribed the officials from Star Medicals to retrieve this information. But the question was if this IDK killer knew that Rajeev would scam the family of Arvind. If that was true, then this IDK killer was trying to completely destroy the family of Arvind. But he didn't do such things with Pankaj or Faisal.

Maybe the hatred against Arvind was more than others. Team Sagar sat in their den.

Jitendra said, "I think this Rajeev guy is stupid, and just trying to play saint. I know how the conscious of these pricks are. He is just trying to cover up his sins by another illegal insider tip."

Ritika chuckled, "Exactly I think we need to arrest him for insider trading."

Jitendra said, "I mean seriously does he not fears the law, for having told us about this."

Sagar smiled, "We got to look into this, what if we hit a jackpot. I think this would be the last thing that IDK killer would have wanted to surface. Maybe in this instance he hadn't covered his tracks."

Jitendra said, "I have already called the IT guy, he will look into the computer of Rajeev."

Sagar said, "Now you are talking."

A wise cop had said, to judge is the work of court, for cops there is no such thing as bad lead. After all these disappointments and a dirty secret which wont reveal itself, finally Team Sagar was working on an illicit inside tip. Sagar was hopeful that it better be the work of IDK killer, so they could get another avenue to track him down. After all this police work, Team Sagar did deserved a break. IDK killer was no saint, and if Sagar was right he was merciless to have dragged the family of Arvind into this mess. But did it mean that Arvind might have done some more wrong than the other two. It could have been the possibility, or was it just like Arvind was the first murder so the IDK killer wanted it to make grand.

All the questions, and there was only one person who could have answered them, that was the IDK Killer. IT officer was looking into the computer, while Sagar got thinking about his son. Sagar felt like a criminal, who would be responsible for his son going to boarding school. What was Arjun's fault, only that he was a son of an over working police officer. The IT officer was soon done.

IT officer said, "The sender of this email is smart, he has used masking software. But fortunately I was able to track the address of the server from where it was sent."

Jitendra smiled, "It is the address of Star Medicals Head Quarters."

IT Officer left while Sagar said, "An inside tip from inside the HQ of Star Medicals, isn't that strange."

Ritika said, "Who could be this man."

Jitendra said, "My bets are, either it is our IDK killer, or an aide to the IDK killer."

Sagar said, "Remember Reshma, we had the same bets when we were chasing down that lead. But still I think we should look into it, it could be worth chasing."

Team Sagar was headed to meet the officials in Star Medicals. Now only these people could have thrown some light on where did mail come from and what person was behind it. The Headquarters of Star Medicals was just a mile or two from Akbar Nagar. It wasn't coincidence. The odds were maybe this IDK killer had listened about this tip in a bar or maybe while travelling in a metro. But then how could he have managed to mail Rajeev from their HQ. This was a big miss fit. The best bet they had was that IDK killer be connected to this email.

Jitendra was driving the car, while Sagar was submerged in thoughts about his son. This entire move of Arjun going to boarding school was a big distraction in this investigation. It was a father thinking about his son, thinking about his well being. For long Sagar had wanted to take up a desk job in Police Headquarters for his family, maybe the time had came. Maybe after this IDK killer was caught, these killings were done, Sagar would volunteer for a desk job and be able to give his son his due time. They had reached the HQ of Star Medicals. It was a huge building, inferring to lots of people inside. Already odds were beating Team Sagar. They were now sitting in the cabin of the Admin manager of the company.

Admin Manager said, "How can we be of help detectives."

Sagar said, "As we said that we are investigating the IDK killings, we have a lead that connects it back to you people. Nothing to be scared of, it is just a routine checkup, and your name wouldn't float in media."

Admin Manager exhaled and smiled, "Thank you for understanding, now what is it that connects to us."

Sagar said, "One of our suspects have received an email originating from a computer in this office, about an inside tip that your stocks will go up as soon as the new cancer medicines will be out."

Admin Manager was shocked, "The tip is absolutely true, but how come it got leaked."

Sagar sighed, "I am afraid that this man could be either the IDK Killer or an aide to him."

IDK Killer is an employee of the Star Medicals. This was the last thing that any admin manager of an organization would want to hear. A killer working in a health care company would be bizarre and destroying. He was terrified even with the possibility of Sagar's statement. Team Sagar was trying to establish the connection of the killer with the organization, the admin manager was listening and peeping out from the window of his cabin. All the faces he could see were ones he had worked with for long and they were all good human beings. Ones that would share lunches, ones that would celebrate birthdays of fellow colleagues, ones that would go an extra mile to maintain the profitability of the organization.

Now this Detective was telling that someone from them was the IDK killer. The IDK Killer who has mercilessly shoved knives in bellies of three men and who knew how many else he was now going to target. This was unbelievable. People at Star Medicals were in the business of saving lives and not brutally murdering them. This was the core culture at this organization and all the people working at Star Medicals were scanned through rigorous background checks. The Admin Manager sat on his chair and gulped a glass of water.

Sagar said, "I know it is not easy to process, but the truth remains the same. Now can you tell us, what people in your organization knew about this new cancer medicine."

Admin Manager said, "Very few of them Detective. In fact this new cancer medicine is not made by us, rather we were in the process of purchasing a patent from a foreign company. This information was only with the management. Trust me detective the people of Management are all nice guys, they would never do such a thing, and seriously just forget if any of them could be the IDK killer."

Sagar said, "But this information did leak, and you can't deny it."

Admin Manager exhaled, "Okay, what do you want me to do."

Sagar said, "I want to question all the people who had this information."

Admin Manager sighed, "Okay, let us wrap this up today itself, and I do not want anybody else to get an air of it, especially media or my junior employees."

Sagar agreed while Admin Manager left his cabin to meet the management people individually. Till now nobody in the Star Medicals had even got a hint that police had arrived in their workplace for investigating the IDK killings. Everyone was working calmly in their cubicles. Sagar was taking every opportunity to glance at every other person working on the floor, maybe to spot a suspicious face, or a dubious individual. But they were all calm like ocean.

How could that violent IDK Killer be an employee of Star Medicals? It was a total miss match. But if IDK killer was an employee of Star Medicals, then he was more dangerous than Sagar had anticipated, because he would have the art of deception. A wise man had said that a person who has multiple identities is the most dangerous man because you never get to know who he actually is. Team Sagar was sitting in the cabin of Admin Manager, while they browsed through the annual employee book of the organization. Sagar couldn't help but stare through the faces of employees in the pictures like if he was scanning every face, while Admin Manager came back.

Admin Manager said, "He is our director, Manish, and was leading that acquisition."

Sagar shook hands with him, "I know this is awkward, but we just have few questions to ask. First, where were you during these dates and times? They are the time of al the IDK killings."

Manish took a look and said, "Well, I was in Paris, have just returned two days back. In fact the company from which we are acquiring these drugs is a French Multi National. I was busy with them doing the paper work. I got to know about this IDK killer after the second murder, when it broke the international media."

Sagar said, "Did you told about this acquisition to some other employees, junior staff."

Manish swayed his head, "Not directly. Look detective, my entire travel arrangement was done by a junior staff. My Marketing team has been briefed that we will be launching new medicine so they better cut off their budget. I mean they are not kids, rather all of them have doctorates to their name. They can guess it by themselves."

Sagar nodded, "That was helpful, thank you for your time Mr. Manish."

Manish had a valid point. Guessing that a company was planning to do something big was not hard, especially when there is a lot of activity in upper management. Sagar knew how gossips worked in workplaces. Sagar never worked in a private firm, but he was connected to people to know how rumors catch fire. The head count of people in this headquarters was over 300, and it was practically impossible to take a look at every individual.

Sagar had kept his hopes very high before hitting this place. After interrogating Manish least one man from those 300 people was off the list of suspicious person of interest. A director of a PAN India company would not sell his honor for few bucks, like Reshma in unwanted circumstances did. Nor was it possible for Manish to be present in Paris and Delhi at the same time to commit these murders. Sagar was getting curious to meet other people too. Sagar was hoping that he got something tangible that could connect this organization back to IDK killer. Finding IDK killer sitting on a chair in this floor was the last hope he had. Soon Admin Manager entered.

Admin Manager said, "He is Vivek, our legal manager. Worry not, he is not here to ask about warrants, but he was one of the key people involved in this acquisition."

Vivek said, "As a legal professional, anything to help you Detective."

Sagar said, "Where were you on these dates, and time. Please have a look."

Vivek smiled, "I was in Ahmadabad for the first two timings, as I had gone to see some legal paperwork for our Gujarat factory. For the third timing I was probably in office drafting the paperwork for the acquisition which has led you here. Yep that is right."

Sagar said, "Did you told anyone about this acquisition in your company or outside."

Vivek said, "Outside no chance, but inside I think you got to understand. See I am the Manager of all legal things in here. I have a team. When drafting this contract, it has been several times seen through the eyes of my team. We all are bound by confidentiality, but things like these can easily catch attention."

Sagar nodded, and he truly was in agreement with the legal manager. This time it was another man off the suspect list. Could a lawyer would take up law in his own hands, let alone be knife. What was worrying Sagar was that the news of this acquisition had already gone out from the hands of the management while it was completely impossible for the Team Sagar to interrogate these 300 people individually. What if one of these 300 people who knew about this acquisition went on to have drinks at a club and spoke out from their loud mouth to have been heard by IDK Killer, or maybe aide of the IDK killer. Moreover in this High Tech world it was also possible to re route that mail Rajeev received from one of the PC's here.

The chain of passing information could have been too long to have been investigated. Admin Manager got couple of more management people who again had the same thing to tell. They had solid alibis and their juniors were always kept in cc when these emails used to travel inside the organization. It was tough to tell who this insider could have been, and it was tougher to assume that IDK killer worked in this place. All the interrogations were done, while Admin Manager had got some soft drinks for Team Sagar. He still had that nervousness in his heart, not for being caught, but for reputation of org.

Admin Manager said, "So what do you think Detective."

Sagar swayed his head, "Your management seems to be clean. But I have this feeling, strange feeling."

Sagar continued, "Can you arrange me a list of people who live in Akbar Nagar and a place to interview them."

Admin Manager said, "Sure, there are some people. In fact there is one whom I think you should look into".

Chapter 14

A wise man had said that most of the battles are fought within conscious, and he was right. The conscious of this admin manager made him finally vomit that there do was a person whom Team Sagar should inspect. Did he over spoke? Could that person be the IDK killer, Sagar didn't knew, but for sure this person must have done something to raise that brow of suspicion. To an extent that Admin Manager didn't even thought of his organization being tainted with the fact that IDK killer or his aide worked here.

In this whole world there is nothing more precious than a human life, it was the mantra that Sagar lived on and he was happy to see that the Admin Manager shared his beliefs. This man whom Admin Manager was pointing to was Naman, he was an old employee of Star Medicals and has shown his loyalty to the organization from time to time. If someone was to see his professional records, which were clean as bleached white, no one could have raised a finger on him. But unfortunately he was also a resident of Akbar Nagar and more importantly his looks were what had made Admin Manager give up. Admin guy was up with his professional file on his computer while Team Sagar watched it in anguish.

Sagar said, "God, how can you be so irresponsible, just look at his face, with all the beard he looks exactly like the sketch we circulated, and don't tell me you didn't saw that sketch."

Admin Manager was dumbfounded, "I am sorry detective, but I couldn't just relate him to being a murderer."

Jitendra said, "Oh really, so what has changed now."

Admin Manager said, "You all are here and there has to be some reason behind it, and he is the only man who pops up when you asked about nearby residents."

Admin Manager said, "But you got to agree with me, that his shaven look doesn't matches with your sketch."

Jitendra was about to but Sagar interrupted, "Okay, okay, lets bury this. Now we have someone, maybe we will be able to save some lives. Where is your Naman, by the way."

Admin Manager took Team Sagar to the upper floor where Naman was seated. They avoided the elevator which opened directly on the floor, and rather took the service stairs. The moment had come, and Sagar was praying that this be the killer, because the window he had were limited and he also got to save lives of people. But could this super smart IDK killer have committed such a mistake of leaving this huge lead behind. He under estimated the friendship of Arvind and Rajeev. He must have considered that Rajeev would never tell anyone that he had an inside tip, as it was illegal in India.

The forces of this world have got all together to change the conscious of Rajeev which led them here. Sagar was feeling a little relieved, because if Naman was the IDK killer then he would not be able to commit any more murders at least under the watch of Sagar. They stood near the stairs peeping from the door into the floor. There it was Naman casually talking with a colleague. How calm he looked. He must have got peace after killing three people. Sagar held the knob on door to push it, while Jitendra restrained his hands. Sagar turned around in amazement.

Jitendra said, "Detective just think about it, we do not have prints, we do not have DNA, we do not have any evidence against him. By confronting him, we will only make him more cautious and a little more provoked. I think we need to take a back foot."

Sagar sighed, "Seriously, after all this I cannot waste time. First at least we got to talk to him, to know if our suspicion is even in the right direction."

Ritika said, "Do you think he is going to cooperate, and we don't have enough for a warrant."

Sagar said, "I do not care Ritika, all I am interested in is saving lives."

Sagar continued, "And if this scumbag is the same IDK killer, then he is going nowhere other than prison."

Jitendra drew back his hands, while he unbuckled the cover of his gun, so did Ritika. They all moved in together towards Naman. Suddenly all the attention of the floor was towards Team Sagar and the Admin Manager who was clearly in a cringe worthy situation. The people on the floor haven't still guessed that it was Police striding into their office, but they have got an idea that something unwanted was in process. Then the eyes fell on the guns they had by the waist.

Naman was still standing and trying to process all of this, was in a little shock. All these people had their eyes on Naman. He drew himself from his colleague, and stood straight. Maybe it were the Health Inspectors that were here to investigate something was all that the floor could think. Admin Manager came in front whispered something in the ears of Naman and they all walked together into the conference room of this floor. Sagar was just trying to catch the glimpse of this Naman, and already his guts were telling him that hey this is the man you have been looking for. They sat in the conference room.

Naman said, "Okay, so you all are policemen, as the admin told me, but why am I here."

Sagar said, "I am sure you must have heard about the IDK killer."

Naman waved his head, "Yes, every other person in Delhi knows about IDK killings. I think he is a monster, who has no heart, and he kills his victims mercilessly. But then I also think that something very bad must have happened to him, to drive him into this madness."

Jitendra said, "Great, you seem to know a lot, despite of the workload here at Star Medicals."

Sagar threw the sketch from Reshma and Naman's picture with beard on the table, "Don't these two faces look familiar, what do you think. By your talks you seem to be highly opinionated."

Naman chuckled, "Seriously, you think I am the IDK killer. Come on I save lives, and not take them."

There was smile on face of Naman which still had that blood on his lips. All his life Sagar had dealt with scammers, robbers, and murderers, and this wasn't new for him. The mere fact that they were still talking had instilled faith in this Naman that the police had nothing against him, apart from a matching sketch. This confidence was visible on his face, and his laugh of mockery was hurting Sagar to a point of being in hell.

Naman took out his phone and without saying a word to Team Sagar called his lawyer. He was no more talking to the police, without having a legal representative by his side. Naman hung up the phone, and tried rising up from his seat, while Jitendra pushed him down to have that tough talk. After mercilessly killing three people neither the IDK killer was going anywhere, nor anyone whom the police might have suspected of being the IDK killer. On the floor, few people were constantly passing by the glass wall of the conference room just to have a peek on what the heck was going on inside.

Sagar placed a paper with times of the three killings in front of him and said, "Where were you on these dates and times. Be sure to give a right answer."

Naman took the paper and said, "I was in my apartment, but I don't have an alibi, though you can check with my landlord who lives just one floor down me. Every time I pass the stairs, he greets me from the open door in courtesy. That is the kind of goodwill I have."

Sagar said, "Did you know any of the victims, Arvind, Faisal, or Pankaj, before the murders."

Naman said, "No, I never even had people by these names in my life."

Sagar said, "Have you ever been to IDK, the Indian Dancing Klub, with a K."

Naman said, "Maybe once or twice when I was a teenager. And look Detective, I don't know where this is going but I am not the person you are looking for. So instead of wasting my time, please talk with my lawyer. Okay".

Naman left while Team Sagar couldn't stop him. The good news was that finally Team Sagar had someone who was awkwardly similar to the IDK Killer, least by appearance. Sagar had a strong gut feeling that their search has ended, and he was the one, Naman was the IDK Killer. Naman might have left the conference room but he was already up in the radar of Delhi Police.

A wise man had said that if you want to catch a monster then better look in the alleys. Team Sagar had left the HQ of Star Medicals while carrying the personal file of Naman in their hands. A patrol car was also stationed outside the office of Star Medicals to keep 24*7 eye on Naman. Now every step that Naman would make would be recorded under the watch of Sagar. If a criminal thinks that they can out smart a detective that has been on the job for more than a decade, then they must have been living in a fool's world. Team Sagar was back in their den, and after a very long they had that winning smile on their faces. It was not a visible smile that adds grace and shine to your face, but they knew each of them had it.

Jitendra said, "He is an orphan, and have lived his childhood years in Kalika Devi Ashram."

Sagar said, "If he is an orphan then whom is he avenging."

Jitendra said, "I don't know detective, but maybe something is missing from this file. This man is smart enough to cover his trails. Obviously he hasn't told this world about his roots, maybe this fire of vengeance is nurturing in his heart right from the childhood days."

Sagar said, "Since when he has been living in that ashram."

Ritika said, "Since he was nine years old."

Sagar swayed his head, "Nine years, and nine stabs in each of victim. This is it. That was what he was trying to convey. God damn it, why didn't it crossed my mind that these blows could be the number of years. Okay, now take me to his home. I know he wont be there, but I just want to see it and our next stop will be that ashram."

Jitendra and Ritika took the papers with all the details of Naman and they were now headed to his adobe. Sagar was just curious and wanted to see the place where this monster dwelled. In police work every single detail counted and his home must have been his base. After all this police work finally Team Sagar had a person of interest with a profound suspicion. All this time Sagar had started to doubt his detective skills, but with Naman entering this investigation, he had his confidence back. It was also satisfactory to see that Naman was just another criminal who couldn't outsmart the police. All those clues of IDK Killer and the over confidence behind it was soon to be vanished.

Sagar just wanted to keep a full surveillance on this man. By the behavior he displayed, it was certain that Naman had panicked. But if he was on a mission, then he would not abort it, but rather kill the last man or the two last men before he got caught. This was the frame when he was likely to do something stupid. Naman knew that police was on to him, so he would be extra cautious. They have arrived at the building where Naman lived. Jitendra pointed towards Naman's flat.

Sagar said, "Okay, so he lives on second floor, while there is a back balcony too from where he could escape our eyes. Jitendra I want you to identify every exit and make our people watch him. In any case he just cannot out smart us now. Enough of his madness"

Jitendra said, "On it sir, I will have patrol team of entire South Delhi be alert on this."

Sagar said, "This place is not very far from the places of all three victims. Makes a convenient spot"

Ritika said, "It is closest to the house of Arvind, the first victim, whom he must have watched very carefully. I mean that is what my intuition says."

Jitendra said, "Sir, Naman has left his office. I know its early, but he called in sick."

Sagar said, "Mark my every word. Do not leave a sight of him."

Sagar couldn't help but notice the surrounding of the place where he lived. There were two gardens near the premises, maybe that was why he was so obsessed with killing his victims near park. It was an old building, but the locality was quite plush. An orphan who doesn't has any family to back up, could afford such a place by compromising the savings he could make. That was odd. This house was like a reminder to him, maybe from the house he once used to have. This building or the surroundings reminded him of something. Killers like Naman always had such kind of outlook, the revenge seekers who keep their wounds fresh. Maybe Sagar was over thinking it, but this place was out of budget for an orphan working in Star Medicals.

Sagar was done and the Team was now headed to the Kalika Devi Ashram. This was the place which might have answers to the questions of Sagar, after all this was the place where our IDK killer grew up. A wise man had said that man is just but a reflection of his upbringing. It didn't meant that Naman was taught how to kill people in this ashram, but sure in his growing years he must have developed that vengeance in his heart. They were sitting with Somendra Sharma, the manager of Ashram.

Sagar said, "Thank you for talking to us Mr. Somendra. We know that you have been working here for last 4 decades, and so we would just like to juggle your memory for a bit. It is about Naman one of your kids who is presently working with Star Medicals."

Somendra smiled, "Naman is a sweet heart, every month when his salary comes, a part goes to this ashram. But what about him, is he in any trouble?"

Sagar said, "We think he might be the IDK killer. For now what is more important is who got him here."

Somendra said, "Stop it detective, he cannot be the IDK killer, for all I know about him. Now who got him here is me, yes I found him sitting outside our ashram, and when I asked him about his parents, he said he was an orphan, so I took him in."

Sagar said, "Did he ever talk with you about his family."

Somendra said, "Never, few times I asked, but he said that as long he remembered, he had no one of his kin around him."

Team Sagar glanced each other, while Somendra went inside his back office to bring the old records and pictures of Naman. Sagar was now 100 percent sure that even at that time this Naman was smarter than the people that surrounded him. A kid can have a brain to sit outside an orphanage, but not know about his family. It wasn't like the day Naman came to this earth he was orphaned, and even if that was true he would have gone to the darker side of the alleys doing drugs and doing crimes.

This man Naman had all figured it out, and all through his childhood he was able to fool this nice man Somendra. Just by sending the ashram money from his salary was not enough to cover up his brutal crimes. The intuition of Sagar was telling him that this woman angle in this investigation was of his mother. This was the best guess that felt appropriate. Somendra came back with a file and two photograph albums. This was all he must have had on this kid Naman. Despite of helping the police, he had a peculiar and disgruntled face. He sat while Team Sagar was already browsing through the papers and pictures.

Sagar said, "Do you remember anything strange from his childhood."

Somendra said, "During his early years, he used to have nightmares that would wake him up in the middle of the night. But that is very normal detective, trust me, I have dealt with many street kids."

Sagar said, "Anything else, his habits or his likeness."

Somendra looked out of the window and said, "He was very fond of parks, and I used to love this fact."

Sagar said, "Did he had any friends in this ashram."

Somendra shook his head while Sagar received a call, "Detective, please come down, Rajeev has created a scene."

Chapter 15

He was very fond of parks, the one statement that had got stuck in the mind of Sagar. Now he knew why this IDK killer aka Naman targeted his victims near park. The mysterious woman whom Naman was avenging must used to take Naman to parks, which he missed the most. It was striking Sagar the most that how could few young kids, Arvind, Pankaj, and Faisal do a harm so extreme to turn Naman into a monster. The only explanation was that they killed this woman, but at such a tender age. All three of them were normal beings as depicted by their family, so could they have killed a woman.

A wise man had said, never believe something unless you see it, or hear it, post which it becomes a fact. Sagar was prepared to forget whatever the families of these victims have said. This was the only way going forward. Team Sagar was now headed to a popular restaurant where Naman usually dined. He was a single man and often went out for dining. Even serial killers do have a life. They were outside the gates, while few policemen were surrounding Naman and the others were surrounding Rajeev. Sagar really wanted to thrash some furniture on the ground in frustration and for the chaos created. He approached to Rajeev, who was still very upset and in profound angst. Team Sagar stood in front of him.

Sagar said, "Rajeev are you completely nuts, I mean what have you done."

Rajeev in an agitated voice said, "Look who is talking, you say I am nuts. You know this man had killed my best friend, and still he is roaming free while a police car is constantly escorting him. What a special treatment it is detective. You know just pardon me one murder, and I will finish this monster here and all."

Jitendra said, "Look who is talking, the same man who tried to scam the dead friend."

Rajeev said, "I learned my lesson, and now the guilt in me is killing me."

Sagar said, "Rajeev this is the first and the last time you have interfered with police investigation, getting it."

Rajeev said, "Got it detective, but don't let him get away with it."

For the first time in this investigation Sagar felt sorry for Rajeev. His guilt has made him loose his cool. Why wouldn't he, Rajeev was the man who got played upon by Naman which eventually led to the murder of his friend. All things said but Rajeev was little over reacting by calling Arvind his best friend. Well that all happens the moment you get cheated.

What happened in here was that Naman was having his dinner while Rajeev got to know about Naman being the killer. Rajeev didn't wasted a second and came walking in straight into this restaurant to thrash Naman. They both had a fight, an ugly fight which also disrupted the interior design of the restaurant. When they both were lifted apart from each other, the situation was that Rajeev was more badly hurt than Naman who only got few superficial bruises here and there. Rajeev had just under estimated the strength of Naman, or maybe his conviction. Sagar was talking with Rajeev, Naman was busy making calls. This was what Sagar was afraid of, and it was happening. Rajeev was now draped with few bandages while the policemen were taking him to hospital. Sagar stopped them to have a little more talk with Rajeev.

Sagar said, "Forget everything, tell me where you learned about Naman that he was the killer."

Rajeev said, "That is not important detective. He is right there, just go and grab him, slam some charges."

Sagar exhaled, "Just answer me, where did you learned about Naman."

Rajeev in a low voice, "I have subscribed to a local news channel on internet. It was from there I received this news story that police is suspecting heavily on Naman for being the IDK killer."

Ritika came in from behind and showed her phone, "It is worse than you think detective."

The news had started to spread, while Sagar exhaled, "Now how the hell did that happened."

Before Sagar could even see off Rajeev, the media people have already started to gather around the restaurant. Everyone had only one question on why did the police thought that Naman was the IDK killer. A person who had risen from the absolute ground, without any family backup to have grown into an educated person to finally earn his living that too in healthcare by devoting his life to the people. Media was seeing Naman as an ideal guy. Many sketch artists have got on news channels to claim that this match of Naman with the sketch by Preet was not exact.

The only thing that Sagar was averting all this time was media attention and attention of the public, and here it was coming from all around the Delhi to overwhelm the situation. Sagar felt angry on what a stupid act Rajeev had done. Just because of his wreckful behavior now Naman was enjoying sympathy of people. A wise man had said, emotions can be disastrous, if they aren't controlled. He was damn right. Team Sagar was now headed towards Naman who was looking fine considering he was the one who got to beat Rajeev. He had that winning smile on his face which invisible to all, but Sagar could see it.

Sagar said, "Naman, it must be a great day, with all that attention to you for being a victim."

Naman said, "Trust me Detective, people like me, the ordinary ones are victim on any given day. I would like to quote you, must be a great day, that now entire Delhi knows that I am the suspect of being IDK killer, the monster who has already killed three people."

Sagar said, "Not happy though, but a little sad that it came out the wrong way."

Naman said, "Oh Detective that grief is just going to increase, because my lawyers have already slammed Delhi Police for defamation charges, harassment charges, and an assault from a civilian because of what you think of me. Isn't it too much, or just a collection of three charges."

Sagar said, "If you are what I think, then you are going nowhere but behind bars for life."

Naman said, "Chose your words detective, my lawyer is standing just behind me. It can be a fourth charge on you."

Naman smiled and walked away while leaving Sagar in a state of angst. When Sagar had not known IDK killer he was assuming that this killer was smart, and now Naman the prime suspect was a living example of how smart people are. It felt like the nightmares were back in this investigation. Now Sagar had to stop keeping an eye on Naman as per the books, but that could have killed every possibility of closing this investigation. Sagar was also sure after this that Naman would not stop, he will strike again, but Sagar didn't knew when, who and where.

Team Sagar left the venue of this dog fight, while avoiding all the questions posed by the media people surrounding his police jeep. Sagar was damning himself on not being able to foresee it. Jitendra was right when he had stopped Sagar from opening that door. It was the impulse of Sagar that led them here. Sagar needed to accept that his sub ordinates could also be right at some point. Now this big mess was all over the place and someone had to stop it. A mess that Delhi Police PR team would take a long to clear up, and by when Naman would have killed all his targets, and probably would also have left the city for good.. Team Sagar was sitting in their den with a disappointment in their heads.

Sagar said, "You were right Jitendra, maybe we shouldn't have confronted him, and kept a close eye anonymously. This entire situation is because of me. Didn't knew that despite being a bad guy he would back fire. Clearly this man Naman has no guilt of killing those three people that too brutally."

Jitendra said, "Don't take it personally detective, we all sometimes make calls that go bad."

Ritika said, "I am sure this tip to media is given by Naman himself."

Sagar said, "Yes that crossed my mind, and maybe if we can prove this, we can nullify the charges made against Delhi Police, and get an official warrant to keep an eye on him."

Jitendra said, "The news channel which Rajeev had subscribed to was Delhi ki Khabar, and the good news is that I have a friend who knows the owner of this place. I think we should hit it."

A wise man had said, that purpose of a man is to walk, while purpose of the god is to pave paths. Just when it felt that Naman was winning this war against Delhi Police, this Delhi ki Khabar struck out as a ray of hope. These journalists have a very high code of ethics when it came to disclosing their leads or informant, but with the jack of Jitendra's friend Sagar was hoping that they would get a hold on some vital information. Sagar knew that Naman for now must have been laughing at the fate of Delhi Police after his master stroke, but he didn't knew that Delhi Police also had a stubborn detective named Sagar.

This time Sagar was taking it personally. Naman had not just only made fool of the Delhi Police but also had proved that its detective whose name was flashing in every news channel was incompetent. This Naman had his hands deep down the throats of all the stakeholders in this investigation. Now it was turn of Sagar to back fire. But how could Naman know that Rajeev had subscribed to Delhi ki Khabar, maybe through his social media channels. That could have been possible, as social media is like an open book. Team Sagar were inside the small office of Delhi ki Khabar. Everyone in their office were despicably watching Team Sagar, why not, these were the people behind the failure of IDK killing investigation. Aditya came out who already had a conversation with Jitendra.

Aditya said, "I am sorry for all those prying eyes, because I know deep down you were doing your job."

Sagar said, "Let's not waste each other's time, I just want to know from where and how this lead landed up in your news room. But please only the truth, because it can mislead the entire investigation."

Aditya pulled the laptop from his bag and opened the email account, "Here is the mail that was sent to me, from one of the official email ids of the Star Medicals. With the kind of authentication it had, I was left with no other choice but to follow this tip and publish that article, which is now viral."

Sagar took the laptop to his face, and the email read like this.

Dear Delhi ki Khabar Team,

I am an avid reader of your news channel. I follow it everywhere, and truly believe that you people are out there to uphold justice and deliver the news that is unbiased. It might sound strange, but today apart from being a reader, I am also going to act like an informant. Yes, something terrible has happened in my office today. The investigators of IDK killing came in striding into my office and told me that one of my staff member is the IDK killer. They matched the sketch that was made by Reshma aka Preet, with one of my colleague Naman and went all hard on him. I strongly believe that sketch was not a match, but still the Delhi Police is blaming Naman for these murders. Personal opinion apart, Naman had an alibi as his house owner, who knew that Naman was in his home while these murders happened. This is a total anarchy by Delhi Police. At that time I couldn't raise my voice, but now I see why, so I could tip this news to you. Delhi Police is just trying to close this case by entrapping an innocent citizen.

I hope you will make this tip buzz around every citizen of Delhi.

Thanks, Admin Manager of Star Medicals.

Jitendra was also reading and said, "That son of a gun admin did this."

Sagar said, "That is what Naman wants us to believe. I am sure he must have made his way around to the computer of Admin Manager, or worse could have hacked into his email account. This could also have been email spoofing, there are lots of software on internet."

Ritika said, "But we cannot prove anything with this, because it seems it comes from the admin guy."

Sagar slammed his fists hard into the table, while he couldn't believe that again this IDK killer had managed to fool the Delhi Police. With a progress of invasion like this, it would be not far from now that a fourth body fell at the hand of this IDK killer. Sagar couldn't have stayed quiet. Team Sagar left, again through the hallway of prying eyes of Delhi ki Khabar staff people. This IDK killer was always ahead of every move of the police. Sagar was now unsure on who was watching whom. At every move Team Sagar was finding defeat.

Maybe Team Sagar hitting the Star Medicals because of that small loophole was also his plan. His plan of a bigger agenda to defame Delhi Police and make the detectives look like sissy girls in front of public.. It was possible, considering how smart Naman thought of himself. A wise man had said, people those who have anger in their heart, cannot make place for others. Delhi police was a force against his mission, so Delhi Police would also have to go down for this man to win. After a long time Sagar was feeling helpless. He had already received calls from his seniors to drop his pursuit against Naman. But Sagar knew by his heart and his guts that this was the man responsible for IDK killings. Sagar parked his car near the house of Naman. They sat and waited for a minute.

Sagar said, "Did you call everyone."

Jitendra said, "Yes Detective, to everyone that thinks blood looks good only in blood banks, and not on streets."

Ritika said, "Well that was little dramatic, but glad to know we still have few good men."

Sagar said, "You know, at this point in this investigation I am not afraid of a backlash from my senior officers, but what I fear is that another person is going to fall down at the hands of Naman. There will be blood, more blood, unless we catch and stop this Naman."

Jitendra said, "I truly agree with you Detective. I also think that our best shot is catching this Naman red handed. With red I do not mean blood in his hands, but while he is about to take out his another victim. Maybe if we can find the murder weapon with his prints on it, it would be a jackpot."

Sagar said, "I am certain that this man would not keep murder weapon in his home."

Sagar was right, that Naman was no stupid to keep the murder weapon besides the vegetables in his kitchen. He would sure be hiding it somewhere nearby and safe, which was also accessible, yet far from suspicion. What if this murder weapon was hiding someplace in the Head Quarters of Star Medicals, maybe in one of their lockers? It was the best guess that Sagar could make. But did it matter, as he couldn't have gone even near to that office, especially after this media debacle. Going to raid the HQ of Star Medicals was just another way of inviting suspension from the job, and turning all dreams of Naman true.

A wise man had said, desires have no end unless you put an end to your desires. Sagar knew it that this IDK murders were like a once in a lifetime mission or say campaign for Naman. Once Naman was done with it, he would go all clean and then it would be even harder to catch this monster. All the time that now Sagar had was now in between these murders. That was the golden spot. Sagar had to do something before desires, or say deathly desires of Naman were fulfilled. A couple of patrol cars stopped just ahead of Sagar. They all stepped down.

Sagar said, "Thank you officers, for taking the call. It takes balls to go against the rules to enforce the law."

An officer said, "Detective I have full faith on you. I believe that Naman is the IDK killer."

Sagar smiled, "But that is not enough, we also got to have evidences against this monster."

Another officer said, "Anything, anytime, just say it detective."

Sagar said, "This could also cost you your job, so you people have to extra cautious. I want you all to be my ears, and eyes on Naman. I want to know about every step he makes, every place he visits, every person he talks to, everything. I want a 24*7 surveillance on him that too off the record. No one can know about this. You all must know this man Naman is very smart. By now he must have figured that we will take a step like this. I am not sure how, but he must have already made a plan to deal with our surveillance. But then we also just cannot stop."

Jitendra said, "We will be available at any time you might need us. I am sure it will take 4 to 5 days, for surveillance, and soon we will be done. But the question is, how, by him winning it, or by we nailing him."

The officers shook hands with Sagar and soon they were off, while one officer stayed in his car near the house. The keep an eye mission was already activated. Sagar received a call from Sarika. It was odd. He picked it.

Sarika said, "Sagar, Arjun is missing, I don't know what to do, just come back home."

Chapter 16

A wise man had said, when trouble comes, all you think about is family. Arjun was missing, and dark thoughts had started creeping into Sagar's head. It was not just Sagar, but Sarika also couldn't stop herself from thinking of the worst. A son of a crime investigator going missing was a red flag. Criminals that Sagar had convicted might now be having a piece of him. Sagar was driving his car at full speed and had even broken a couple of traffic lights. Could Naman be behind this, of course he could have been, especially after Sagar taking so much of personal interest in this IDK killing investigation.

Anything bad could have happened to Arjun. If Naman was behind this, then all Sagar hoped was that Arjun didn't become his victim or say an avenue of collateral damage. Apart from anger in his head, Sagar was also feeling helpless. He knew Naman was smart, and very dangerous. His hands won't tremble before hurting Arjun. The rage Naman was carrying inside was too dangerous for people that he hated. Arjun could have become a victim of that rage. Sagar had reached his house, where already few police vehicles were on standby. Sagar rushed inside his house, to only find that Sarika was sobbing while she sat on the couch. This was the moment which every policeman was wary of.

Sagar said, "Hey, be strong, now I am here, nothing will happen to Arjun I promise."

Sarika in a trembling voice said, "What if something had already happened to him. Sagar it is all because of you, your job, that now our son is missing. If something bad happens to him, I will never forgive you, and this will be the end of our marriage. I no longer can live in fear."

Sagar said, "Hey calm down, its okay. Where was he last seen."

A policeman intruded, "At his school, where somehow he sneaked under the eyes of watchman. It has been exactly 4 hours since he was last seen."

Sagar turned to Sarika, "Did you contacted his friends."

Sarika said, "All of them, in fact his class teacher has contacted every student in his class. Nobody knows where he could be. This is all my fault, today I just got a little late in picking him up."

Sagar was already gritting his teeth. What scumbag would have done this, surely someone with bitter face off with Sagar. All he could think of was Naman. Sagar picked his cell phone and called the Officer who was keeping an eye on Naman on directions of Sagar. The officer told him that he had gone out to Azad Nagar for some grocery shopping but then came back and now was in his home. The nightmare had just turned real, Azad Nagar was the same place where Arjun's school was.

All of a sudden Sagar felt losing control of his body. As if he would just faint, and pass out for a while. His feet were loosing the hold on the ground beneath him. If anything, I mean if anything bad had happened with Arjun, Sagar sworn to himself that he would kill that monster right on this night. Sagar patted on Sarika's back while he gestured Ritika to comfort her, who had also came down listening to the missing news of Arjun.

Sagar took Jitendra with him and was already on his way to confront Naman. Maybe days of this monster were over now. He should have never dragged the family of Sagar into this. It was his biggest mistake. Sagar was standing at the doorstep of Naman with relentlessly ringing the doorbell. The door opened.

Sagar said, "Listen you wretched soul, if anything had happened to my son, I will come back and put a bullet or two right in your head at point blank. I don't give damn to what would happen to me. Now spill up where my son is."

Naman smiled, "Detective I haven't studied law, but I am sure that right now you have breached least a dozen of them, and still you call yourself a police detective and the IDK killer as a monster. I understand that when it comes to family, we all go crazy, and do stupid stuff like threatening people or killing people. But the good part is that finally I am a little happy to see that you do share some beliefs with me."

Sagar was losing it, "Where is my son. I am not going to ask again."

Naman smiled again, "If you think this is done by the IDK killer, then your son must be in some park."

Sagar held his collar, "You better start praying for your life right now, where is he."

Naman said, "Come on not only IDK killer likes park, but some fathers, sons like it too. That's all I have to say."

Naman slowly pulled the hands of Sagar from his collar and went back inside while gently closing the door. Something struck Sagar and he straightaway went back to his car, to drive towards Azad Nagar. Damn this Naman was now playing games with the police. Where did he got that balls from. He was no longer scared of what police repercussions would follow. The fiery detective of Akbar Nagar Police Station was now praying to gods in his thought, one thing he never did, just to ensure that his son was safe.

Sagar was driving the car at top speed. For the first time he didn't care if he was a detective who had just broken a law by threatening Naman. For now he was a father who was praying that his son didn't got caught up in cross fire of this investigation. Sagar was blaming himself for this. Just because he was a policeman, with a brigade of officers under his command, he still didn't had rights to give living nightmares like these to his wife. All this police job had given him was a bitter relationship with his own wife, lesser time with his own son, and also sleepless nights. He reached the Azad Nagar Children's park, and strode inside to only see that a boy was sitting all alone on one of the benches. He approached with heavy breaths and sat beside him.

Sagar said, "Son are you okay."

Arjun turned, "Dad what are you doing here. It was supposed to be some quality time alone. Oh I get it, I am late for home right. I was just about to leave."

Sagar tightly hugged him and said, "Don't do this ever again. You know how worried your mom is."

Arjun said, "She is always worried dad, tell me something I don't know."

Sagar noticed wrappers of some chocolates and said, "Who gave you chocolates, and how come you are here all alone for last 4 hours. Were you with someone."

Arjun said, "Come on, you don't know. It was a friend of yours who took me from my school, he even had a badge. He was nice man, he knew I was going to boarding school, so he took me here, for me to enjoy some quality time being free before I go to that prison. He was a big fan of yours, and complimented me for being smart, and brave. We talked a little and then he left with a goodbye kiss. I thought you must have sent him, didn't you."

Sagar are still blowing heavy breaths. This Naman was now a pain in the back. How could he have dragged Arjun into all of this? Most importantly he knew that Arjun was going to a boarding school. This man not only had eyes and ears on the victims, but also on the family of investigating officer. This was not it, Naman also had a fake police badge. He was more dangerous than Sagar had anticipated. Sagar felt thankful to god for having found Arjun unscratched from the perils of Naman's hatred.

This night had become unforgettable. Not everyday Sagar felt on edge of losing his only son. In his head he had already made a promise to himself that he wont be leaving Naman any time soon especially after this reckless act of his. By dragging Arjun into this abyss of danger, he had only caused bigger problems for himself. This investigation now would not stop till Naman got behind bars. Sagar again hugged Arjun as if it was the last day of his life. Somewhere down in his heart this was a reminder to Sagar on how important his son was to him.

Sagar said, "How many times have I told you, to not talk to strangers. This nice man was an imposter."

Arjun felt back, "You mean he was a bad guy."

Sagar said, "Let's not get there. For now this is your last night of being schooled from home. Tomorrow you will be gone to a boarding school, let us have this moment. In fact let me treat you. You want some more chocolates, or maybe ice cream. But wait, lets first tell your mom that you are okay."

Sagar sat with Arjun, while Sarika also rushed in to meet them. Soon all three of them were sitting on the bench. This moment was never going to come back again, so they felt every bit of it, of being a family together.

A wise man had said that the only thing which holds us best is the family. In this moment Sagar didn't care if Naman was making plans to hit his fourth target. Sagar didn't care if he had threatened Naman despite of the warnings given by his superiors. Sagar didn't care if Arjun had made a huge mistake by not only meeting with a stranger but actually to have walked with him to this park to eat chocolates given by the same stranger.

Sagar just wanted to seize this moment, between a small family he had. For the first time Sagar, Arjun and Sarika were in one frame with smiles on their face. Didn't knew about Arjun who was still a kid to think about these aspects of life, but Sagar and Sarika were feeling grateful to god for bringing them together, for being there as a shadow wherever they went.

It was morning, and after a long Sagar went up to the boarding school with Sarika to leave Arjun. Somewhere deep down Arjun was actually excited to be in this new place, and this feeling was making Sagar contended for the moment. Sagar and Sarika were now returning back, and were in their car together.

Sarika said, "So finally I can have my breaths back without having worrying to pick and drop Arjun from literally every where. Don't know if I should be happy or sad to see Arjun go to a boarding school."

Sagar said, "You made a right choice, with our working lifestyle it is barely possible to look for Arjun."

Sarika turned her face, "No hard feelings, right. He is also my son."

Sagar smiled, "Not even an inch of it. In fact after yesterday I think I need to be present for Arjun more frequently. Let's make a deal, from now on, all the free time of Arjun will be divided between me and you by 2:1. I think you have already done a lot for him, and now it is my chance to be that good father."

Sarika shrugged, "Only if you can live up to it."

This was a calling from above, and Sagar knew that he had to answer it. If Sagar had given enough time with Arjun, there wouldn't have been a need for him to look for a shoulder in Naman, be alone even if he was a criminal who had plan on intimidating Arjun. If only Sagar had taken up the responsibility of least picking Arjun from the school, this wouldn't have happened.

Sarika did a fine job in picking Arjun from school, but many a times she got late because of her hectic work schedule. Sarika was not to be blamed for that. It had to be Sagar to stand up in all those times. Meanwhile they were driving, Sagar realized that after a long time he was with Sarika and there was no bad air between them.

A wise man had said that there is no glue stronger than grave times in sticking up the family together. Maybe Arjun's disappearance from the school was a blessing in disguise. Sagar had left Sarika at her workplace, while she actually smiled before getting off. Was this all real, Sarika smiling at Sagar and not giving chills. A day has never been better than this with Sarika, least in recent times. Sagar was back in his den at Police Station and was sitting with his team. The agenda of catching Naman was still up.

Sagar said, "This man is wicked, see how easily he had dodged our officer to sneak and get Arjun to that park. This is a clear signal that he is going to strike again, but who, when, where, is all I am unable to figure."

Jitendra said, "I still am unable to understand, how Arvind, Faisal and Pankaj were connected."

Sagar said, "Hey do you remember Pankaj being anxious and his father noticing that he might have known the two."

Jitendra said, "Which means that the fourth victim must also have known by now that he is next."

Ritika said, "But then why isn't he coming up to us."

Sagar said, "I don't know, maybe a hitch, maybe he is hesitant, or maybe he is uncomfortable in disclosing the sin they all together had done with Naman. Anything could be possible. But if he is not reaching out to us, let us extend a hand, maybe he will open up. Jitendra call a press conference, that too right now."

A press conference and a public announcement was now the only hope that Sagar had. If Naman could depend on the power of people, then why cant Delhi Police. Sagar damned himself for not having taken this step before. But still it wasn't that late, Sagar could have least saved a couple of lives. The only worry Sagar had was what if this fourth victim didn't showed up despite of public announcement. This was the case same with Pankaj. He was not stupid, he knew that IDK killer would come for him. But maybe it was the guilt of the sin that he had done in past had stopped him. Sagar was just thinking on what sin could group of kids do to drive this madness.

The reporters had started coming in, much before than the police staff had anticipated. A news about IDK killer was just irresistible for any media person especially of Delhi in current times. On the other hand, Sagar was certain that after this press conference Naman would become more cautious, and maybe even more provoked. Just like every other decision of life, there were upsides and downsides to this one. What actually mattered was that Sagar was willing to take this chance. He was facing the reporters in the conference room of Akbar Nagar Police Station.

A reporter said, "Can the police department answer on why they have been harassing the upright and innocent citizen like Naman, whose fault is to have a face matching the sketch."

Sagar said, "I hate to tell this to you, but I wish that victims were someone you knew personally. Despite of the great public pressure of leaving Naman out of this, I still receive calls from the families of victim on why we are not pursuing charges against Naman. It's not like they want to grab everyone by the back who is a suspect, but because they trust Delhi Police, they trust me, which is not the case with Delhi Media."

Reporter said, "Back it up with an evidence, and we will trust you more than our jobs."

Sagar smiled, "I shouldn't but I want to. The tip about Naman being a suspect that went to media came from an email id of Star Medicals. Now you tell me, whom do you want to trust."

The chit chatter in the conference room grew, while Sagar interrupted, "I have called you all for something very important. Maybe we can save a life or two. We know that IDK killer is going to strike again, and we also know that the fourth victim knows what is coming. But for some reason he is scared or feeling embarrassed. We urge you all to tip us if you know someone like that. If any person watching this feels that they could be the fourth victim, then show up, and we will protect you with our lives. The IDK killing hotlines have opened again. Thanks for cooperating people of Delhi."

Sagar left while leaving behind hordes of journalists posing questions at him. Soon the news started catching fire, and this press conference had hit at the right spot. The damage was done, while the all news channel were airing this revelation in their prime time slots. There was no chance that the fourth victim hadn't seen this or hadn't heard this. Now all Sagar could do was cross his fingers and wait for this fourth going to be victim to show up. The victim now had to choose between his embarrassment of revealing truth or losing his life.

What was stopping this man or maybe a woman from coming up front and expose this IDK killer. Keeping quiet at this time was stupidity and a self lethal act. Sagar was in the room with officers taking up calls on hotline. He was personally monitoring the process. The idea was to not leave any space for error. The calls had started pouring in. Just like every other police campaign, they were receiving many irrelevant calls, that had nothing to do about tip, but asking about who this IDK killer could be, or asking about if his neighbor could have been the IDK Killer. Then a call got forwarded by an agent to Sagar.

Citizen said, "I am very scared that this IDK killer will kill me."

Sagar said, "Hey sir, do not be scared, did you knew the first three victims."

Citizen said, "I have seen them all, at some point or the other in my life. See I also live in Akbar Nagar."

Sagar said, "That is not enough sir, did you knew them in person."

Citizen gulped his saliva, "Hard to tell, but I also live near a park."

Meanwhile an officer came running from behind, "Detective, IDK killer has done it again. The fourth man is down."

Chapter 17

A wise man had said that a criminal never stops, he only takes breaks. It was true and IDK killer has struck again to claim his fourth victim. The fear of Sagar had come true. The press conference might not have led to the unmasking of this fourth target, but it surely did provoke the IDK killer to kill his fourth prey. This was not just the fourth murder it was a defeat of Delhi Police which was working relentlessly to catch this killer. Ironically the crime scene was victory park. The linguistic expert was right.

Only if Sagar had given him his due attention this murder could have been averted. Sagar was expecting this IDK killer or Naman to execute this fourth hit near to his home. This was the reason why he had beefed up the security near Naman's house. Sagar was wrong. Maybe Naman made a change in his plan. Everybody knew that Victory Park was huge, and already had many police officers guarding it, or patrolling around it. It made it a less likely venue for a murder. Maybe Naman took the advantage of this fact. The entire crime scene was surrounded by people and police. There was a sheer discontent in hearts of people, as they saw Police with demeaning eyes. This IDK killer had stolen the show. Team Sagar was standing near the body. It was hard to see another man lying dead for reasons still unknown.

Sagar said, "Damn it, didn't I told you all to keep a close eye on Victory Park."

The officer in charge said, "Detective, you also told us to keep an eye on Naman's house."

Sagar said, "I am assuming you are not the only person who patrols the Akbar Nagar Police Jurisdiction. Don't you have junior officers who probably could have been deployed here. This murder is clearly the failure of not our intelligence but diligence. If only you would have done your job, maybe we would have the killer in our hands."

Jitendra intruded, "Hey Officer, just secure the perimeter, lots of people are crossing the police barricades, and we also need to protect the crime scene from getting contaminated."

The officer left while Sagar said, "Hey, I was still talking to him. God this is all on us."

Jitendra sighed, "Detective calm down, it is not only his fault, and people are watching us."

Sagar waved his head. The disappointment of this murder had clearly taken over the conscious of Sagar. The first murder, Sagar couldn't have done anything. In second murder, Team Sagar was unable to decrypt the IDK, and it happened. The third murder, they had some ideas about the venue, but again it happened. Now before this fourth murder they had diligently followed the clues and had even cracked them, but still the fourth victim was lying dead.

Sagar had also shared the list of possible locations of the fourth strike with his seniors. Now what was he supposed to tell them, that despite of Victory Park being the number one spot for fourth strike, they still failed to protect this man from being dying. Wait, not just from dying, but dying of brutal blows of knife to his belly. If this information got leaked, Delhi police would have another PR disaster. The police officers in the crime scene were already looking for clues, while sniffing dogs were doing their job. Sagar came close to the dead body while another officer joined him. If any normal person would see this dead body and the deathly bruises, he would faint to witness the brutality of a heartless killer.

Sagar said, "Do we have an ID on him."

The officer said, "His name is Rakesh Jaiswal, resident of Akbar Nagar. He has a showroom of garments in the area."

Sagar said, "Do we have any witnesses, or anyone that saw him coming to the park, or maybe anyone that saw Naman or the person resembling our sketch leaving the park."

The officer sighed, "None Detective. This area of the park is the most deserted one, as you can see there are wild bushes growing up in these patches. Barely people walk up till here. Though there is a gate just behind us, which could have been the entry and exit point. That is all we can infer for now."

Sagar said, "Any murder weapon, or any trace left behind by the killer."

The officer said, "None that we can spot, but the forensics team are on it. The MO of this murder is the same, and I am afraid we are going to find any trace, just like the prior murders."

Sagar took a deep breath, while he couldn't stop the smell of blood going up through his nostrils. At last another family man was down, another family man had became victim to this IDK killer. It was unjust, no matter what had happened to Naman in past, but he didn't had any rights to murder someone. There was a whole legal system in place. This Naman should have come to the police, and see lawyers in court if he wanted to get justice.

A wise man had said that crime is like a disease which catches up too fast unless you have a strong immune system of character. Any person who would have been in Naman's place who had spent his entire childhood in an orphanage, would obviously think of getting justice the rowdy way. But was it right, never in a million years. Sagar was headed to the wall to see what clue IDK killer had left this time. It was becoming like a ritual with a man down and a clue up for who is going to be next, or rather where is it going to be next. Sagar hated every bit of it, not because he didn't liked challenges, but this was all like a game, a bloody game where people were losing their lives. This was what disgusted Sagar the most. They were standing opposite to the wall.

Sagar said, "URS, nice way of saying yours. So now it spells like, I don't know but I am yours."

Jitendra said, "Detective, also there is a full stop after URS. Does it means that the killings are now done."

Sagar said, "I hope so, because I am not liking this bloodshed. Plus now the sentence, or the message is complete. It makes sense now. This probably is the last of IDK killings, which makes me fear. Phew, it makes me fear that this IDK killer aka Naman is soon going to vanish from this city."

Jitendra said, "I feel the same. If this is the last killing, our chances of catching the IDK killer have already gone slim."

Ritika said, "But he has already left another clue, this got to mean something."

Sagar said, "This only means that he is winning it, nailing it, and killing it."

Team Sagar left the crime scene, while Sagar was still feeling like the culprit, the culprit because of whom this murder ever happened in the first place. Such a solid piece of lead, but still Sagar was unable to save Rakesh's life. This was troubling his head. This IDK killer was getting on the nerves of Sagar. This Naman was constantly giving uncomfortable vibes to Sagar. Having known that a particular person is behind a series of crime, but not able to do anything because of lack of evidences was the most frustrating situation that any detective could face

Sagar was feeling like a kid, who was being constantly bullied by this criminal. Despite of the fact that Sagar was the one who actually held Naman's collar and threatened him to death, he was still feeling like a kid, a helpless kid with no one to look up to. A tougher task was awaiting Detective Sagar, which was to meet the family of Rakesh. This was what always gave chills to Sagar. Facing family who had just lost their bread winner just because police was unable to do their job was a tough and shameful spot. Team Sagar had arrived in the house of Rakesh. Clearly this man had big bucks, but also a sin from the past which Sagar was still to find out. Team Sagar was standing with wife of Rajesh, Riya.

Riya said, "Please do not say anything, I know police is trying their best, but still it was their incompetency to have saved my husband. I have heard about all of your stories on News channels. I know that you are sorry, but what I also know is that you are not sorry enough."

Sagar exhaled, "I have already given my words to three families, and I am giving it to you too. This case is not shutting down on my books, till I have that IDK killer behind bars."

Riya said, "Just stick to it what you have said."

Sagar nodded slightly, "Any enemies Rakesh had, or anything from the past that was troubling him."

Riya said, "He was very closely following the IDK killings. At time I even thought of asking him, and eventually I even did, but he said nothing and just that these IDK killings were interesting."

Riya took an excuse of a moment to see a relative dropping by, while Team Sagar waited for their questions to be answered, though Sagar hadn't expected anything new. What he had expected and what he was used to was hostile eyes. Yes the people that have visited Rakesh's house were constantly staring Team Sagar. Sagar could never understand, when will normal families learn to see policemen as humans.

As per the current conventions, every Indian family saw Policemen as corrupt, soulless, and people without integrity. Sagar was used to it, so he didn't care, instead he used the opportunity to roam inside the house and actually see the place where Rakesh lived.

He couldn't resist from taking close look at pictures of Rakesh hung in the living room. There was one also from his school days, but sadly the uniform was not even a close match to that of St. Mary's. The biggest question again popped up, where did the hell these four victims became friends. Then there were some sport trophies kept in a cup board that clearly had Rakesh's name. He was athletic, and it was also obvious from the dead body he had seen. Still he succumbed to the blows and force of Naman. Sagar was just trying to make himself at home when Riya returned back, but this time with some cups of tea.

Riya said, "My father in law wanted me back in his room. He told me to request you people to please discharge the body, quickest possible. I hope I am not asking much, and probably this could be the least you can do apart from catching the IDK killer."

Sagar nodded, "Sure, now when was the last time you talked with Rakesh."

Riya waved her head, "Every time he walked out of the showroom he gave me a call. Today was no different. I hate to say this, but my husband had a drinking problem, though I was very clear that he cant drink in our house. So he always resorted to the Grill House Club, which is situated very near to the Victory Park, and did his thing, before he came back home. Today too he went there."

Sagar said, "Was he accompanied with someone, maybe a drinking buddy, or some new friend."

Riya shook her head, "No, he went there alone, and when he partied with his friends. It was mostly at their houses, as his friends didn't had a problem from drinking at home, or say their wives were probably more cool."

Sagar blew his breath, "We will be in touch Riya, and trust me, this IDK killer is going nowhere."

Team Sagar left, while Riya was all left alone with hopes that she would get justice. Sagar didn't said it, but with every murder he was getting disgusted at the acts of this IDK killer. Hatred for Naman was just going up in heart of Sagar. This IDK killer had already ruined three families, considering Faisal didn't had kids nor wife. It were three families where children would grow without a shadow of a father. It were three families who have lost their bread winner. It were three families, that would have widows. This IDK killer had no right to do this.

No matter what crime they had committed, there is always the right way to get justice. Sagar couldn't get the picture of Naman out from his head. That face laughing at Sagar, laughing at Delhi Police. How calm he was when he was hinting that he had met Arjun. Sagar didn't knew the difficult past he had, but now this Naman had became a cold blooded psychopath and nothing else.

A wise man had said, never trust a criminal, because they trust no body, and trust is a two way thing. Sagar couldn't understand why even Rakesh was hesitant in coming up to police. His interest in these IDK killings was now not coincidental, he was part of these killings, and he must have known it that the Killer was coming for him. Team Sagar sat in their den, while the autopsy guy Nitin came in with his findings.

Sagar said, "I am guessing that it is the same weapon, same knife that killed this guy Rakesh."

Nitin said, "You are right, but one thing is sure new for you. The number of knife blows in his belly were 10. Its like a pattern, 9 then 10, then again 9, then 10. I am not sure what it means, but the killer is sure trying to convey something which we are missing here."

Sagar said, "That is interesting, but we already have many clues to decipher, so this pattern is in a long list."

Nitin said, "The victim was intoxicated with alcohol. There was significant amount of whisky he must have drank, to an extent that he must have been incapable of walking straight. Plus this whisky was been drunk by Rakesh voluntarily, by taking breaks. You know what the drill is with drunkards."

Sagar said, "Yeah soon we will find that out, on how the whisky was consumed."

Jitendra said, "The car is waiting detective to our next stop, Grill House Club."

Without a wink Sagar walked off while Jitendra and Ritika followed. This Grill House Club was a quite high end club with members only entry. Rakesh sure had a great deal of money for being a person who visited this club regularly, that too just because he couldn't drink at home. The question was what person had walked Rakesh to the Victory park. Rakesh had his own car, and no way he would have stopped randomly on the street to walk down to Victory park especially after he was so drunk. This could have only happened if someone from the club walked with him, though the car of Rakesh was found parked outside of the club. The parking guy of Grill house club had bluntly refused that Rakesh driven inside the club with his car.

The question was why would Rakesh park his car outside and then walk inside the club on foot. A person like Rakesh, who would usually drink alone, why would prefer walking amidst the crowd to enter the club. This entire story only indicated that someone was with him before he entered the club and after he exited it. Clearly that one person could have been Naman, but as per the officer keeping an eye on him, Naman was at his fitness club. Team Sagar was inside the club and talking with the floor Manager, Akash. He was pretty cooperative and was spilling everything he knew.

Akash said, "Detective the last thing I want is my club to be defamed with this murder. I request you again to please keep our name out of your public statements. It will be a huge favor, especially after all the cooperation I am giving you, this is the least we expect."

Sagar sighed, "You are such a fancy place, and still you don't have CCTV at entrance or parking. How come"

Akash shrugged while his junior came back with a drive, "Detective this is the entire CCTV footage of the day, of course from the inside." Akash then played it on his laptop at the counter.

Sagar couldn't believe his eyes and banged his hands on the table with Akash left scared, "Damn, that is Naman, just half an hour before Rakesh hit this place, and last time I checked Grill House is a club and not a fitness centre."

Jitendra said from back, "I had my doubts about the officer."

Akash said, "He came in here alone and walked out of here alone, just like I said before, and as you can see the entire video, except our waiter nobody came even close to Mr. Rakesh." .

Sagar wanted to thrash this piece of electronics, not because he didn't get anything from it, but because he saw the face of Naman. Could this be a coincidence, never in million years. The worst part about this revelation was that despite of this video Sagar couldn't even have got an arrest warrant issued against Naman. This was the legal system of India mocking Sagar and his intuitions backed by facts. But if any Judge or the jury could have only seen through the eyes of Sagar they wouldn't have even one doubt that Naman was this IDK killer.

Sagar enquired about Naman, as this was a Members only club, to which Akash told that Naman had joined recently before a month. All this was happening under the nose of Sagar and once again this Naman had managed to make a fool out of Delhi Police. They were out on their way from the club, while they stood at the entrance.

Sagar said, "Naman could have avoided that CCTV footage, but he didn't. You know why? Because he is mocking us, he thinks he is the smartest man in the room. And who is this officer keeping eye on Naman. Such a fool."

Jitendra was quiet while call came to Sagar, "Detective, we have missed a life saving call from Rakesh."

Chapter 18

A wise man had said that human life is nothing but a never ending quest. He was right, even after we die, our afterlife quest starts to be remembered in memories. Memories of Rakesh were not fading away any soon. He might have gone, but his eternal presence was still being felt. People of Delhi still had fresh memories of Rakesh in their conscious. For them a one of their own was murdered. For them a regular human being trying to meet his ends on a day to day hustle was gone. How strange it is, that we people always find something or the other that resonates our lives with others, yet we are called just bunch of individual people. This is what makes us human beings, and not a human being.

People of Delhi have come together to ward off their only enemy which was this IDK killer. Sadly Naman was not that enemy of the people, as they saw him as a victim of Delhi Police incompetency. Sagar was now headed back to the Akbar Nagar Police Station. It was a terrible failure of Delhi Police intelligence and Sagar was just praying that the media didn't get an air of this, or this would be another disaster. Sagar entered the Hotline Department of the Akbar Nagar Police Station, and the faces of the Junior police officers were telling the entire story of great police disappointment.

Officer said, "I am extremely sorry detective, but we couldn't just identify if the threat was real. It appeared to be one of those bogus calls, and moreover Rakesh didn't said anything solid, for us to take that call seriously. I know it is our failure, but we are not alone in this fault."

Sagar exhaled, "You know what, you all are going to lose your jobs, and take away mine too. So this better stays between us, no one can know about this call."

Officer nodded, "Yes sir, this stays here, and is going to die here."

Sagar waved his head, "Play the recording, I want to hear it. After all our hotline call might give us some clue."

'Hello, my name is Rakesh, and I fear that my life is in danger. Why do you think that sir? I know it, I am going to be the next target of this IDK killer, I just know it. Did you do something bad with him? That I cannot tell, anyways, I didn't do any bad to him, but someone he knew. Did you knew the other three victims. Listen I am not in a mood to tell you a story, just know that my life is in danger? Sorry sir, but you are not giving us vital details of this threat, so I will have to hang up. The line dies.'.

Sagar said, "God Damn it, I want to thrash this Naman. Wait maybe I should."

Sagar left the room while Jitendra and Ritika followed. The ploy of opening the hotline did really worked, but it was the weak conversation between Rakesh and a junior police officer that couldn't help him. If Rakesh had only told that he knew the three victims personally, Delhi Police might have been able to save his life. Not just save his life, but could also catch Naman by his tail. This was not just a disaster, but a very unfortunate event. Rakesh did was scared of losing his life. His modulating voice and trembling words depicted that. He wasn't just scared but even made this call which would have been a tough take, but the poor choice of words, and maybe his insecurity of revealing the wrong he did, cost him his life.

Sagar was in his cabin, and he called Sanjay. Well Sanjay was not any police officer. He was a local mobster of Akbar Nagar. Desperate times needed desperate measures. After all these years situation came when Sagar needed a help of a mobster. Sagar was keeping his calm, but from inside he was fighting a battle. He was not sure if he was doing the right thing, because if anything went wrong Sagar could have lost his job. There was right, there was wrong, and there were things that needed to be done. He trusted Sanjay more than his guts. Sanjay with two of his body guards came in to meet Sagar. He was happy that Sagar called him.

Sanjay said, "Detective, detective, detective, it is so nice to see you after this long. I cannot express how happy I am that you called me personally and not sent some warrant. I am sure there is something I can do that you want. So tell me, how may I serve the officer, who is responsible for downsizing my gang to one third."

Sagar smiled, "You must have heard about the IDK killings. We have a suspect, in fact I and my team are sure that he is the one, but he wont confess, so I want you to give him a little treatment."

Sanjay said, "Naman, right, I see the news. But what is in there for me."

Sagar said, "Your brother Sunil, who is battling drugs possession charges. I will get them dropped".

Sanjay smiled, "This Naman must be someone very special. All the time I have known you, you never took favors from people like me. Anyways, consider it done, that too by evening."

Sanjay was walking out while Sagar said, "You will just be doing some good, and yes Naman is special, because he has murdered four of my fellow citizens."

That was Sagar speaking his heart out. This was no longer the game of Police Versus a Criminal, but this was a personal calling for Sagar. The promises he had made to the four families of the victim, he had to up keep them. In his mind Sagar had made a promise to himself that he will bring down this IDK killer aka Naman no matter what it takes. If this time Naman walked away freely, it would be death of Justice for the people of Delhi. It doesn't just ended here, there will be more people like Naman who would come up and take law and order in their hands. At any cost Sagar had to stop Naman and his Doppler effect.

The wounds of those dead bodies that Sagar had to see, were still flashing in his head. Those cuts were like a reminder that Sagar had to do more, hustle more. The confidence that Naman had whenever he came across with Sagar was still echoing in his mind. It was killer confidence or say confidence of a killer. This man needed to be stopped. He might already have with that full stop after URS. But he also got to come under the justice system of this city. For the first time Sagar was seeking favors from people he wanted to be frightened of Law, just for Justice to prevail. The plan was simple to terrify Naman, to an extent that he confesses. Sagar wanted to make sure that Naman got his message that Sagar would not let him live peacefully for the rest of his life.

Jitendra said, "Detective what are you doing. We have already been warned to stay away from Naman, and now you are ordering an assault on this man. Don't you remember what he did with the media coverage when we accused him of being the IDK killer. This time he will simply go nuts."

Sagar said, "I no longer care, all I want is this man behind bars."

Jitendra said, "Detective, I hate to say this, but you are taking this too personally."

Sagar said, "Four people have been murdered under my watch, now how do you want me to take it, professionally, intellectually, or factually."

Ritika said, "I am with you detective, this monster needs to be caught, at any cost."

Sagar turned to Jitendra, who was feeling defeated with this argument, "Fine, you have my vote too."

Naman was a big man. He was self independent, and a successful professional. He was not only mentally strong, but also physically. This was why Sagar chose a mobster to beat the shit out of him and not just some thug. Sagar knew that Sanjay would be a perfect fit for this job. He was not just any mobster, but the most infamous mobster of Akbar Nagar. Chances were very high that Naman would have heard about Sanjay and might also know him by face, which was enough to instill fear in him at the very first glance.

All these years as a detective, Sagar had learned one thing that criminals also had normal people aspiration, and they also want to lead a normal life. Sagar was trying to hit at this very sweet spot. He was hoping to make the every day life of Naman a bit more difficult to an extent that he did something stupid and got caught. Sanjay and his four men were sitting in their SUV just outside the house of Naman. They were waiting for their prey, while Naman didn't even had a clue that this was going to be a tough night. Like every day, Naman got out from his house to buy groceries. Sanjay and his men came out with cricket bats and starting beating the shit out of Naman. Soon Naman was bleeding.

Sanjay said, "Naman, nice name, but nicer would it be to call you the IDK killer."

Naman said, "Listen man, I got no beef with you, so stay out of my business."

Sanjay exclaimed, "Oh so you agree that IDK killings are your business. That is a good start, because you have just killed four people I knew. Yes, not only you knew them, but I knew them too. You see, this is my area, this is my jurisdiction, not the police type, but the mob type, and now you have breached my territory. We have a problem. By the way do you know who I am."

Naman spoke softly, "Yes, you are Sanjay, and you own these streets."

Sanjay took his bat and hit hard at his back, "Good, oh that was my gesture of saying good. So now you understand one thing, that I am going to make your life hell, unless you confess to your crimes and are put behind bars. Trust me, what we did to you today is what we call starters, worse is about to come. Got it? I said, Got it."

Naman with a trembling face said, "Yeah, got it, got it."

His face was bleeding, he had bruises on his body, maybe he had got a broken bone too, considering the intensity of the blows of those bats. Naman could hardly stand on his feet, so he dragged himself to one of the benches just outside his house. He gathered all his courage and sat on the bench. Had Naman expected this, maybe somewhere deep down in his heart that too, to be hit by the police and not the mob.

Mob has no rules, mob has no mercy, mob is not answerable to anyone, maybe that was all the idea of doing this. Naman sat for a while trying to catch up his breath. For a minute a shiver spread across his body for fear of collapsed lungs, but there it was a huge breath, and he felt alive again. A wise man had said, choose your friends closely, and choose your enemies even more closely. Naman had no doubt that the person behind this beat up was Sagar. He was the only person most pissed on IDK killer not being caught. Naman smiled to himself and pulled out his cell phone. Yes he has saved the number of Sagar, just in case, and nothing to do with friendly vibe. Naman was not sure that will he be even able to talk to Sagar or not, but there was something more powerful that was driving him. He called Sagar.

Naman said, "I am sure Sanjay must have updated you. But this is a reminder that yes you won for now, Happy."

Sagar smiled, "Happy, huh, seriously Happy with you getting beaten up. What should I be happy about that you killed four people and are just beaten up for that whose bruises will vanish in a couple of days. No Naman, you didn't get me. What I am feeling right now is the tip of the happiness. What will make me happy is you standing in a courtroom getting defeated, and spending rest of your life in prison, where inmates will teach you a new language."

Naman chuckled, "Detective, I was in pain, I am in pain, but for days to come I will no longer have to feel this."

Sagar said, "Listen you prick, I don't know what god you believe in, but start praying."

Naman said, "Pray, huh, seriously pray to god. What should I pray to god for, for giving me an orphan life. If that is the case Detective, then you too don't get me. I do not pray to god detective, I only pray to ones I love, and they are gone, and none of your police work can bring them back. All I can say for now is that you are stupid, huh, you are stupid detective, that is for you too."

They hung up the call, while instilling anger in head of Sagar, not because Naman had called him stupid, but this was again one man mocking the entire justice system of Delhi. Sagar had encountered criminals more dreadful and more ugly than Naman. But there was something about this Naman which was getting on the nerves of Sagar. For starters, hardened criminals rarely make normal middle class peace loving people as their target, but Naman was doing exactly the same. Hardened criminals are scared of losing their lives the reason why they are always hiding, but this Naman was roaming all free and to top everything was contacting press to be seen as innocent man. Hardened criminals are barely educated which is one of the reason why they become criminals, but this Naman was highly educated, and maybe saw himself above the lesson of humanity. These reasons were just a tip of what was annoying Sagar to its core. To topple everything this man Naman actually had the guts of calling Sagar right after he was beaten up. What was that for, just to say that hey I am still standing and not scared of what Police might do next. Team Sagar was sitting in their den.

Sagar said, "Jitendra, did our linguistic expert cracked what this URS mean."

Jitendra said, "Though it's a simple casual word in English which probably means Yours, and the entire sentence also rhymes well, but still the expert is on it. But what is the matter Detective, you don't look happy. The images of Naman which Suraj had sent were heart breaking for sure. Wait, bone breaking for sure"

Sagar said, "U are stupid, that is what this URS mean, and he said that to me too."

Ritika said, "Damn this man has balls, but then I and our entire team would love to break those."

Sagar exhaled, "What I was fearing of, might happen soon. Yes we had a conversation, and it felt like our Naman is going out of city, not to celebrate his victory, but forever, least for the time being. He is smart, he is strong, and he is also educated. I wont be surprised if he begins his new life within a week of shifting."

Jitendra said, "Got it Detective, we need to buckle up on our efforts."

With this Jitendra left the cabin of Sagar along with Ritika. The conversation with Naman had ended a while ago, but his words were still echoing in the heart of Sagar, you won for now. Was this the only victory that Sagar was going to have in this IDK investigation. A victory that too taken by unlawful means, a victory that was taken with a help of a mobster, a victory which was to make Naman feel a little pain just like his victims had felt.

All his life Sagar had been the good cop, but suddenly after talking with Naman he started to feel the opposite. Sagar was positive that Naman's next move will be to move out of Delhi, and if he did it this investigation would be over in no time. Delhi Police had no solid evidence despite of the fact that they have examined four crime scenes and torn four dead bodies. The statistics were loud and clear that this IDK killer was going to go free. The promises that Sagar had made to the families of the victim were now floating in his head. Had he failed? Sagar was a man of his word and it had suddenly started to feel that this time his promises would become void and hollow. He was clearly feeling lost, by all means, when a call came in.

Sarika said, "Entire Police Dept. knows that you are a man of your words. I hope you still are."

Sagar said, "Glad that you called, I was desperately wanting to talk to a homely voice. Ah, anyways, how are things at office, as this is quite an odd time for you to call."

Sarika said, "Hey everything okay, because you don't seem like you."

Sagar said, "Well, everything will be okay, all I can say. Just a bad phase and bad day in office"

Sarika nodded, "Okay, but that is not an excuse to go and meet your son Arjun before he goes off on a vacation. Yes their new school is organizing a trip, I am not sure what it is about, but just go there and give your son a good kiss, and talk with the teachers. It is now your turn."

Sagar smiled, and hung up the phone. What could be more refreshing than seeing his son's face after such a dull investigation yielding failure. This is where family always beats the odd. Sagar was feeling happy already. He straightaway walked out of the police station and got in his car to drive to his son. It was a long drive so Sagar immersed himself in the memories of his son. Seriously now how grown was Arjun that he was going on a trip without his parents. That will give him confidence to beat the bad days of future. Sagar was already at the Boarding school. There was a whole line of kids with their parents. Arjun saw him and came running, and her teacher followed.

Sagar said, "Hey champ how are you, feels like ages since I saw you."

Arjun said, "Can't believe it dad that you actually made it to my school."

Sagar held him in his arms and talked to the teacher, "So what is this trip about, where are you taking them."

Teacher smiled, "This is a part of our personality development program, and this is not a trip, but we are taking them on summer camping. There is a very popular camp site named, Saint Mary's".

Sagar interrupted, "Saint Mary's."

Chapter 19

That was the name, Saint Mary. Sagar didn't had to stress himself to remember where before he had heard this name. A significant part of the investigation was revolved around this Saint Mary. All this time Sagar had thought that Pankaj talked about the Saint Mary School, but it was now he realized that it could have been this camping grounds of Saint Mary.. It made perfect sense, a summer camp where all these four met, made friendship and did something terrible. All this time Sagar was unable to connect these four together at one place and it was now because of his son Arjun that he finally got his answer.

Arjun going to the boarding school had turned out to be a blessing in disguise. Teachers of Arjun did an excellent job of organizing this trip. Sagar wanted to thank them for the crack they had given in this investigation. Sagar couldn't hold his excitement and at the same time he damned himself of not having thought this. If Team Sagar had looked for other establishments named after Saint Mary he would have got this lead earlier on. A wise man had said that people do not get lucky, they get what is meant for them. This IDK killing investigation was bound to be solved. Sagar had picked Jitendra and Ritika and was already on his way to this Saint Mary Summer Camp.

Jitendra said, "What was so urgent Detective, and I also see that streak of happiness on your face. Why wouldn't it be there, as you always ignore your family, and it is when you meet Arjun this happiness walks in. How is he, and how is the new school."

Sagar smiled, "He is doing great, and so is his school. They are taking him to Saint Mary."

Ritika interrupted, "Saint Mary, why would a school take its student to another school, maybe some fest."

Sagar said, "This Saint Mary is different, it is a summer camp ground. Getting it"

Jitendra was taken back, "So there is a summer camp ground by the name of Saint Mary, damn, this is the place where all four of them met, over a period of maybe couple of weeks, the reason why nobody knew about their friendship. More over they did something bad and forgot each other. Damn it."

Sagar chuckled, "Don't be in haste, it is still a theory, which will unveil itself in max an hour."

The level of excitement was spurting out of the faces of Team Sagar. It was an excitement moving beyond the speed limit of the highway. Just when Team Sagar had lost hope that they would catch this IDK killer, this big lead came in. If now anyone argued about the existence of god in front of Sagar he would give up a fight. The faith of Sagar had just got strengthened. As things were getting unfolded this IDK investigation was becoming more interesting.

A summer camp friendship, then a sin, and then forgetting about each other.. Damn this was why all of them never met after that summer camp. The connection that was broken off between them might have been the reason why these four were hesitant to come in front of the police. It was the guilt. It was all making sense. This was why Naman was so confident that police would never track down these suspects to Saint Mary Summer Camp, because no police officer would think like that and no family of victim would find it mention worthy. Meanwhile they have reached Saint Mary Summer Camp, as written on the entrance it was a 90 year old establishment, right from the British days. The camp was huge, and all Sagar could see was greenery all around. They entered the office of manager and were seated with him. The Manager's name was Anil.

Sagar said, "We are from Akbar Nagar Police Station. You must have sure heard about the IDK Killings. We are here following a lead and hope you could help us. We believe that all four victims, Arvind, Faisal, Pankaj, and Rakesh, met each other in this camp. We would like you to check the records for us."

Anil skeptically said, "Is this camp in some sort of trouble."

Sagar said, "Not at all, as we said we are following a lead, it is just a routine check."

Anil gestured his peon to bring some files while he attended Team Sagar, "IDK killings, seriously, do you think one of the kids that attended our camp is behind this. God if that is the case, I think we need to be more selective on who comes to stay in our camps."

Sagar smiled, "Anil you are getting on the wrong patch. There is nothing wrong about your camp, nor the policies of your camp. It is not in your hand what kids who visit here do in the future."

Anil nodded, "Yes, you are right, meanwhile let me show you the camp site."

Sagar didn't want to but Anil insisted. The camp site was really big and was a living testimony to its heritage. There were huge halls with beds lined up, then there were halls for the teachers, then there were playgrounds with all kinds of equipment for an outdoor adventure. There was an open air auditorium. There was a huge mess where apparently the food was being cooked. For now keeping aside the investigation, Sagar was pleased to see the camp grounds, considering he was also a father whose kid was about to come here in a few days.

A wise man had said, that we all are born same, but we die differently. He was damn right, it was nothing bad about this camp site, but then you cant control what goes in the mind of the kids that come here. He had also sensed the agenda of Anil behind taking him to see the camp. Anil didn't wanted bad publicity for the camp. Even one news article that IDK killer was from Saint Mary Summer Camp would have destroyed their reputation. After hearing such news, no parent would send their kids here. Sagar was well aware. They were back in the office of Anil, while Peon had got the relevant files.

Anil flipped through the pages and took a deep breath, "It seems that you are right. All these four victims were part of a summer camp in here. See here are their records. In fact they shared the same dormitory with beds besides each other. No wonder if they made friendship."

Sagar smiled, "That was helpful, and we will need a copy of these records for the proof."

Anil said, "Anything to help the police."

Sagar said, "Was there any act they did during that summer camp, an act that might have caused disciplinary action. Any mischief, or any major violation of code of ethics, something like that."

Anil said, "Well there is nothing that indicates any such act in their records, but there might be one person who can help you. Joseph was the supervisor over here during this summer camp, and I know him that he knows every kid that comes here. He is retired now, but I am sure his memory would be crystal clear if anything happened."

Jitendra said, "Where can we find him."

After retirement Joseph had bought house just near to the campsite. Often he would come to visit the camping grounds and feel nostalgic. Anil didn't gave them the address, but instead called Joseph to come and visit the camping grounds. The idea was clear that now Anil was curious about the involvement of this camping ground in the IDK killing. It wasn't like if Anil was an avid follower of murder investigation, he might have been, but here he just wanted to save the reputation of Saint Mary Summer camp. Sagar didn't care if he would have to go and visit Joseph, or if Joseph would have to come here and visit Sagar. The idea was to crack this investigation and for now hopes were stuck on this Joseph.

The worst possibility was that these four victims when as a kid did something in this camp that never came to attention of the supervisors. It could have been the possibility, but by seeing the investigation it hinted that someone might have died because of these four kids and things like that do not go un noticed. Team Sagar was waiting for Joseph. Then he entered, an old man with wrinkles on his face, big beard, and brown complexion. He was skeptical to meet the police, but he sat calmly.

Sagar said, "Nice to meet you Mr. Joseph. As Anil might have told you that we are here for IDK Killing investigation, we would like to have your co operation. I just want you to juggle your memory, and remember if you recall anything about these four kids which now are deceased."

Joseph nodded, "Anil, this is 9109 batch right."

Jitendra interrupted, "Damn it detective, the number of blows, that was what he was trying to say."

Sagar nodded while Joseph continued, "The thing is, my memory is fading away. I would have never recognized these kids, but all I know is that there were few kids behind a very heinous act that happened in my summer camp. Now I know the kids behind it. Wish I had known before, this would have not happened, even if something happened, it would have happened very differently."

Sagar said, "Well, you sound very cryptic, I need you to be clear, there are four murders that have happened."

Joseph smiled and said, "For that you will have to come with me."

It was official that something terrible had happened in this camping ground. Anil who was unaware of all of this was still in shock to hear something disturbing like that from Joseph who was regularly a jovial person. He tried following Joseph and Sagar, but Ritika requested him to be seated in his office while they went off. This was larger than the reputation of Saint Mary Camping ground. With what Joseph was suggesting, it felt that this investigation was not only about four dead people, but about five dead people. Sagar was feeling just a step closer to wrapping this investigation, an investigation that he was taking too personally, an investigation that has gone on his nerves.

Team Sagar followed Joseph who was now entering the archive rooms of Saint Mary. They entered a library, where on one side there was a wall hung with hundred of pictures. Joseph stopped at the first one and glanced at it very carefully. Sagar could see the young Joseph in it. This picture might have been least 20 30 years old. Joseph had moist eyes. He walked further, taking closer look at every picture. He was trying to find a picture. There were hundreds of them but Joseph was patient, and finally he stopped at one picture, where again Sagar could see Young Joseph. He pulled the picture out from wall and pointed to a woman in picture.

Joseph said, "That is Neetu. She used to work here, and was once my colleague. But sadly she is no more."

Jitendra interrupted, "Did she had a son named Naman."

Joseph smiled, "Naman yes the name is right, but he was not his son, but his brother, kid brother. Neetu and Naman had lost their parents when they were very young to an unfortunate car accident. Neetu was everything that Naman had, but then she too was gone."

Sagar exhaled, "Tell me in detail Joseph, what happened with Neetu."

Joseph dragged a chair and sat with the picture on his lap. He took a deep breath and said, "Everything was fit and fine at Saint Mary. Kids used to come here, and leave with memories of lifetime. But then came the batch of 9109. At the same time Neetu was about to get married to a young and successful man. Any man would go gaga over Neetu. After all she was one fine beautiful woman. Few days passed of this batch, and one day I found Neetu Crying in her office. I asked her what happened, to which she said, that her nude pictures were taken while she was bathing in the staff quarters, and few kids from the camp were behind it. Now they were blackmailing her to sleep with them, or they would make posters of these pictures and stick all around the camp. I was furious, but Neetu decided not push this further, as they were just kids. Some days later, I found Neetu covering her face. She was hiding her bruises. I knew she was about to meet her fiancé in Indian Dancing Klub, but then what happened was what I was curious about. Apparently these kids have stolen the address of Neetu and sent her nude pictures to her fiancé and everyone she knew they could get hold of. That was it, she was shamed beyond any limits. See detective those times were very different and she couldn't handle the shame, and committed suicide by cutting her wrist from a kitchen knife. Now I know that she must be resting in peace because of IDK killer."

Sagar felt running out of words, but he held himself and said, "This was indeed sad, and shouldn't have happened in the first place. Thanks Joseph for your testimony, but you will have to come with us to the police station. We want your statement to be recorded officially."

The investigation was cracked open. It was Naman and only Naman could have done this, after what happened with his sister. Team Sagar now could have connected Naman to this murder investigation directly, though they still didn't had proof that Naman actually committed these murders, but still it could have been the start of nailing this man.

There was an awkward silence between the members of Team Sagar. It wasn't like if they had not expected something ugly to be revealed, but still hearing the story from Joseph had for a moment evoked some sympathy for Naman. Any person who would have been in Naman's place would have got disgusted from what happened to Neetu.

These four kids actually demanded Neetu to sleep with them, at such a tender age. Considering that Neetu was like a teacher to them and they actually blackmailed her to sleep with them. To top everything they broke off the marriage of Neetu and shamed her in front of her family. This was not mischief, this was a sin. Maybe somewhere deep down in his heart Sagar was glad that these four got what they had deserved.. But that didn't mean Sagar would not pursue Naman for these murders. They were in their car headed to Akbar Nagar Police Station. Seeing the awkward silence, Jitendra thought of breaking the ice.

Jitendra said, "And we thought only Naman was the monster in this investigation."

Ritika said, "Yeah, I agree, these four were no less than devils own kids. I mean nudes, blackmailing, and then breaking of a marriage. This is just too much. Actually Naman was giving us clues all the way, right from Ishwar Das Kashyap, to 9 10 and 9, to IDK, to letting Pankaj type that Saint Mary, and of course the biggest of them by leaving abbreviations for his next murder. I think he wants the world to know his story."

Sagar said, "Couldn't agree more, but remember, we are still away from convicting Naman for these murders. We sure have connected them all, but still no evidence that Naman committed those murders."

Jitendra said, "You are right detective, maybe we can extract a confession from Naman, after all he wants his story to be heard. I think we can cut some deal."

Sagar said, "All I can say is that it will not be an easy road."

If Naman really didn't care about being caught, he would have leaked the story of his life to that press outlet and not have tipped them about being harassed. The agenda of Naman was very different. He wanted the world to know his story, then he wanted the world to take his side, and eventually be seen as a person who did the right thing. This was the master plan of Naman. He wanted justice but by his own way. The saddest part of this investigation was that if this story of Naman came out then majority of the people would have taken the sides of Naman. To an extent that even relatives and family member of these four victims would also have taken the side of Naman. Such was the profound sin that these four had committed.

Team Sagar was in the Akbar Nagar Police Station. The news of statement of Joseph had already reached the police headquarters and even to Akbar Nagar Police Station. Team Sagar got a standing ovation for cracking this investigation. As Team Sagar passed the hallway there were policemen clapping on this feat. Sagar couldn't help but smile to that honor being bestowed upon them. They were inside the cabin of Sagar while other policemen had got on to bring Naman for questioning after an official arrest warrant was issued in his name. Sagar was sipping his coffee when Jitendra came in.

Jitendra said, "Bad news detective, Naman is missing, possibly leaving the city."

Ritika said, "I have checked with his office but he has already resigned. He has also received full and final from his office. Some colleagues told that he had got a new job. We have also checked at his apartment, but he has left the place, and was seen hopping in an intercity taxi."

Jitendra said, "You were right that he was about to leave the city. I am afraid he might leave the country too, though I have send some of my men checking the recent VISA's issued to find any trace."

Ritika said, "Again he is a step ahead of us."

Sagar said, "Don't worry, I know where to find him, just buckle up and get a back up team ready."

Chapter 20

No matter what hatred Naman had for these four victims, but there also was love for his sister that was driving all this madness. Leaving Delhi would mean leaving all those memories behind. Sagar knew that Naman would want to feel closer to his sister before leaving the city. For the same purpose he had got extracted the address of Neetu and Naman's old house from the Saint Mary's Summer Camp. This time Sagar was one step ahead of Naman.

Team Sagar was headed towards the house. This house was also in Akbar Nagar Police Jurisdiction, and obviously this house also had a park just opposite to it. This was the house where Naman was born into and had spent his childhood before he went to the orphanage. Sagar was sure that Naman would come to pay visit to this house before he left. He might have been a criminal, but the force that was driving him to do these crimes was emotional.

Team Sagar had reached the house. It was in a very bad shape, a locked house which clearly shouted from its appearance that no body had lived here in ages. There was a taxi waiting outside the house, and it was no brainer that it was of Naman. Jitendra even asked the taxi Driver, who was en route to Bangalore and was hired by a man named Naman.

Sagar said, "Jitendra, Ritika, you both cover the back exit, I am going in."

Jitendra in bafflement said, "No Detective. He could be armed, he could be dangerous. We should wait for the back up. I shouldn't be the one to remind you, but he has cold bloodedly killed 4 people."

Sagar said, "He is done Jitendra. He has no beef with me, if he would had, he would not have spared Arjun. Moreover even I am armed, and trained enough to pull down a man who is a threat to me. We cannot take chances of him getting away, so go now and cover the back exit."

Jitendra said, "Okay I am going to back exit, but Ritika you go and secure his cab."

Ritika said, "Yeah, after all you have got some tickling brains despite of the situation. Good to see that."

Sagar said, "Hey, both of you, just secure the exits, okay."

Sagar didn't had to break a lock, or make a forceful entry as the door was already opened. This was the time Sagar had been waiting for since from the start of this investigation, the joy of having caught the IDK killer. It was known to Sagar that he didn't still had any evidences that proved Naman killed those people, but still a joy was a joy. A wise cop had said that deep down all good cops are same, they just want to nail the criminals.

Here it was a little special for Sagar as a cop, as this was no criminal who got swayed away by his mood or emotions before committing the crime. But IDK killer was a deliberate planner, and a sharp minded fugitive who has left all the officers of Delhi Police pondering on how to catch him. Sagar made a move. The house was in condition to fall down to ground at any time. There were spider webs, there were nests of pigeons, there were rats, there was dust that had covered every inch of the house. Sagar heard a sound of someone talking. He slowed down his steps to walk even more carefully with his gun pointed towards his line of sight. Sagar could clearly recognize the voice which was of Naman. But who was he talking to. Sagar saw someone standing in a room and he strode with his weapon high in air to enter it.

Sagar said, "Your game is done Naman, we know about Neetu."

Naman smiled back, "Must say, you are good detective. I didn't hope that you will get here. Anyways now as you are, what are your plans. As I see that you only know about Neetu, but you still don't have any evidences against me, or else an entire brigade of Delhi Police would have been here to arrest me."

Sagar said, "F you Naman, you think you are smart. Then listen, Delhi police is smarter than you. We have managed to find out Neetu, so we will also manage to find evidences against you."

Naman shook his head, "No no, its not F you Naman, Its F for F you Faisal. Yep it was Faisal who took those pictures of my sister, one woman who meant everything to me."

Sagar relaxed himself, "Look Naman, I am not a moral judge of your character, but the fact is that you have killed four people, and you got to admit it and face the consequences, the easy way. Or the tough way would be, that we make you spill the truth out and get you maximum sentence."

Naman said, "You think you are a good negotiator, but do you know me well Detective."

With this Naman took out a knife from his jacket, probably the same one that he had used to kill the four victims, least it had the same make. He put his knife on his neck, while Sagar got alerted to pull back his gun to point at Naman. This was what Sagar was fearing. In the first place he decided to enter the house alone in haste just because something like this could happen. This was the reason why he left Jitendra and Ritika out of the house.

Sagar had known Naman enough that he would not fall prisoner to Delhi Police. The abbreviations that he left on walls were not to gain popularity but to get into the conscious of the people, let them be the judge. Acts of Naman were for higher calling. Sagar knew that Naman would rather die than getting charged with murders. Not because it was a crime, not because the consequences of this crime were grave, not because he didn't like prison, but all because in his eyes these murders were not crime but an act of justice.

Sagar lowered his weapon, "Easy Naman easy, let us talk. See I am lowering my weapon, now you do the same, and let us talk like civilized men. You are an educated man and you know that judge after hearing your story will sure show some leniency in your case. Trust me."

Naman said, "Why don't you start with some leniency and let me go."

Sagar exhaled, "Look, I cannot do that, I am just a police officer, doing my job."

Naman smiled, "Do not stress yourself detective, I knew your answer before me asking the question. The point is that yes I am educated, educated enough to not fall into your trap."

Naman looked up and then said, "I don't know but I am yours sister."

With this he used blunt force to cut his neck, the blood spurted out in a moment, and Naman was fallen on ground in no time. Sagar immediately called for an ambulance but he knew that there would be no saving Naman beyond this. IDK investigation was over. Sagar had also recorded all of their conversation on his smart phone, yep that was being smart of him, to least make his case in the official report that it was Naman who killed those four. Yep those four was the right word which Sagar thought of, because the act they did, was so heinous that it would be a shame if Sagar spelled their names knowing it was for them.

Delhi Police officers have arrived at the scene and the place was now flooded with officers, media and even the neighbors. Sagar finally felt relieved that this city will no more have to a see another murder with an English lesson waiting for them. Deep in his heart Sagar was feeling sorry for Naman. No kid in this world has to go through this, but still his means to get justice were so unlawful. There was something wrong with the justice system of this country, of this city. Only if the investigating officer of the death of Neetu had looked beyond a suicide this would never had happened. Then Naman would have grown to become even more successful person who had left his past behind. Team Sagar had just briefed the officers about the incidence and stood near the house seeing other policemen in action.

Jitendra said, "Another feather in your cap detective, you have closed the IDK killing investigation. Probably the most hyped serial killings in the history of Delhi."

Sagar exhaled, "Wish I could have caught Naman alive."

Jitendra said, "Come on detective, he killed himself, because he knew that he deserved nothing better than that especially after killing four people."

Sagar said, "You don't get it Jitendra. The idea of the justice system is to bring balance in this world. I wanted Naman to be alive to see his court room trial, so later he could realize that what he did was wrong. And that my boy is the purpose of justice system which becomes a precedence for all who take law in their hands."

Jitendra blew breaths, "Detective I am out of here, maybe you should too, and have a drink over this victory."

A wise man had said that past is like a fungus, because if you allow, it grows all over you in a bad way. The investigation was over, and as days passed people of Delhi got over these IDK killings. People of Delhi have seen so many crimes to remember them all. The best part of this IDK killing was that finally people came to know why Naman killed those 4 people. Yes it was the foremost wish of Naman for people to know his story, and they did. Not only people learned about Neetu but they also sympathized with Naman. People of Delhi were no longer going to remember Naman as a serial killer but as an outlaw who sought justice in his own way.

There was some more good that Naman did before leaving this world. The house where he was born and the house where he died, was named to the Kalika Devi Ashram. It was the last time that Naman was getting there to pay a visit to his childhood memories. That was Naman whom people loved briefly, to an extent that some of the neighbors of these victims even boycotted the families of those four. World is a very strange place, and it was so true, some people were hated for killing people, while some people were loved for the same act. Sagar's life had again returned to normalcy, for now he was investigating a robbery case while he was getting late to his office.

Sarika said, "You will never change Sagar. Work has been always more important to you than your family."

Sagar said, "Oh please stop it, now what did I do."

Sarika said, "Its not about what you did, but what you are not going to do. I have already reminded you two times in this week, that there is a function at our son's school, and you got to be there, but here you are loaded with your gun and badge, ready to save the world."

Sagar exhaled, "Damn I am sorry, but can you please go this time, I promise I will be there for the next one."

Sarika said, "Tell me something new, and Sagar you are not keeping your words, remember you promised."

Sagar said, "Okay, okay, I will go. Of course a cultural event in school is more important than missing 15 million rupees. Wait, the school event is more important than two people dead because they came in way of a robber. Robbers can plunder their one more target while I clap for my son. I think Arjun understands my job more than you do. Least he wishes this city to be crime free."

Nothing that Sagar said changed Sarika's stance, while she handed him the keys of the car. Sagar went on to hop in his car to take a different route other than Akbar Nagar Police Station, to head towards his son's school. Even after keeping your children in boarding school the responsibilities of parents doesn't ceases. Sagar was remembering his own childhood where his father even never saw where school of Sagar was. By that parameter, Sagar was way better father than compared to his own. Arjun was doing well in studies, he had great friends, he was fit like anything, what was the reason for Sagar to worry. He was a father of a champ, who could take care of his own. The best part was that Arjun never complained on why he was being pushed to a boarding school, rather based on the previous visits it seemed he was enjoying his days.

Sagar was stuck in traffic and it was long queue of cars before he crossed the signal. All Sagar was worried about was getting late, not to his son's school, but after returning from the school to police station. Meanwhile a call came in.

Officer said, "Detective, I don't know who did this, but there is a dead body here with same MO and few abbreviations on the wall. It's another M for Murder."

From the same Author

One Night Stand

Man Enough

Fuck You Boss

Georgetown

Influenced

Bad PR

Crowd Sourced

Good Job

Can you catch me

**Available on Amazon,
select bookstores, flipkart, and more.**